Children of Violence

A Novella by

Children of Violence
© 2020 by luke Gherardi

ISBN (Print): 978-1-09832-119-2
ISBN (eBook): 978-1-09832-120-8

for makayla

Prologue,

Ron

We robbed a bank. A fucking goddamn bank.

Brilliant.

Have you heard of Guatemala? Teacher says it's far away. Central America? Can you go there please? I won't tell Daddy.

That's the first thing she said to me. Seemed like an odd thing to say. Just a young kid. I guessed she was about eight.

It was a strange moment in time. Something I think about every day. The one wrong decision in my life that spiraled into the hell of my existence today.

It was there, right then, my defining moment.

I was pulling a stick up job at this bank downtown and everyone was on the ground. Everyone except for this pretty little girl. She had a soft smile. No fear in her eyes. Her mom kept trying to grab her. I yelled at them both to get the fuck down. The mom stopped moving and hunched back down. She knew a big dog when she saw one.

The little girl, though? Not scared at all.

I should have listened to her.

I should have walked out right then and there.

Guatemala sounded nice. Still does. Maybe it had beautiful beaches? Maybe I could have found a local gal. She wouldn't speak any English, but I'd learn enough Spanish to get by. I was good at math. Maybe we could have opened a shop. Bought a nice house by the beach. Had some kids. Maybe two boys. I always liked kids. And a girl. I would have named her Annabella. Maybe she would have had my mother's eyes.

This all sounded so great. Wonderful. Grow old in the tropics with the good weather and a woman on my arm that loved me. A true family. Like I never had. Like I never will.

A dream.

A fantasy that never even had a chance.

I didn't listen to the little girl. That little red-haired girl in the polka dot dress that still haunts my dreams. The dreams that could have been.

Or did she have brown hair?

As I wheel myself around the nursing home I wonder how I made it this far alive. Sure, life was always hard being disabled, but now that I was older simple tasks were much more difficult.

I needed the nurse to help me go to the bathroom and couldn't bathe myself anymore. I was so weak. Just a ghost of the memory of my former self.

In my school days I could run a mile in six minutes flat, sometimes a bit faster. Now I have to push a button so the nurse can push me to the cafeteria to get breakfast.

So Ramon and I walked into the bank dressed in our Sunday best with handkerchiefs on our faces.

We found out about the job from Henry. I was new in town and fell in with a pretty good crew. He was the bartender over at Smiley's. He always had a scam going on to make some quick dough. This score was different, though. This was big time and for a street hustler like me, I was all in. Henry had a guy inside the bank that tipped him off the day and time that the bank had the most cash.

The job was simple. In and out.

Sounded fun to me. I was 56 at the time. Wasted my whole life drinking and gambling. Never really could hold a job; never really cared to. Wild and dumb as hell. The only thing I cared about was pussy and quick cash. And this score was going to be my ticket in. Henry said my cut would be up to sixty thousand dollars. I've never even dreamed about that much dough.

For four minutes work. It doesn't get better than that.

And Ramon? He was a man on a mission. So serious. He only was 35 at the time, but sure didn't look it.

About a year before our heist, his wife had committed suicide. Blew her melon out with a .357 magnum down by a lake. A couple of kids found her face down on the bank with half a head. The fat kid pissed himself.

At the time, Ramon was at work, unaware of what had happened. Unaware that there were any problems at all. Life seemed pretty normal. He was a good husband and she was an even better wife.

He was successful in real estate and she kept at home staying busy with projects within the community.

They never had children. Maybe they couldn't? I'll never know.

When the police showed up at his office he wasn't all that concerned. Surely they had the wrong person. Someone who looked similar, perhaps.

But not his wife.

That morning they had made love. They cooked breakfast together. She picked out his favorite tie. He finished his coffee, kissed her goodbye, and walked out the door.

The last kiss.

When he realized it actually was her he collapsed. He aged fifteen years overnight. Bags formed under his eyes. Grey hair within the month.

So many people showed up to the funeral to offer support for him and her family. Neighbors, co-workers, and church members spent time with him after the burial. They all tried talking with him and brought him home-cooked meals.

But eventually time moved on. Everyone went back to their own lives. Ramon sat in his shell of a home, broken and alone.

Why he turned to crime? I think he wanted to die, and he *did*, but I'll get to that later.

So there we were, seven or eight years ago, locking the front doors to the bank after we walked in. Ramon fired his revolver into the ceiling. I told everyone to eat dirt. Everyone hit the deck. A few people screamed.

Except for her.

I didn't notice her at first. My head was throbbing, heart was beating out of my chest, breathing erratic.

Not my first bank job, but definitely my last.

I was worried about a hero. Some cowboy showing up trying to stop us. I played the moment over and over in my head the days prior to the stick up. I was ready to plug a motherfucker. Or so I thought. Such a tough guy back then.

Henry's bank friend filled his bag up with the dough. Ramon cracked him in the mouth to make it look legit. Almost knocked him out by accident. I had a few smaller bags. The teller cried as she filled the first bag. Wouldn't stop shaking.

We were in control.

I felt a tug on my jacket. I turned and pointed my gun. It was the little girl. Her mother screamed. The teller began to fill my second bag. Tears were streaming down her face. And that's when the little girl told me about Guatemala. Told me she wouldn't tell her daddy.

The teller dropped some of the cash. I told her if she did it again I'd drop her like a hot rock. She tried to keep her composure but couldn't stop shaking.

The little girl tugged at my jacket again.

"Hey mister, can I pray to Jesus, please?"

What?

I told her to get down. She didn't need to pray and I wasn't going to hurt her. She looked at me again, but this time confused.

"I don't need to pray for me." She looked down.

"I need to pray for *you*. I'm scared for you."

My bags were full. I paused. I asked why she'd be scared for me.

"Because Daddy is mean."

Daddy is mean?

"And I don't want him to hurt anybody anymore."

She looked down, with sadness on her face. Her mom whispered loudly, "Gracie! Be quiet! Get down, now!"

"I heard Daddy tell Mommy he was all done working for Mr. Kearney. No more hurting people."

Her mother yelled, "GRACIE! GET DOWN NOW! QUIET!"

She finally listened. She ran around the counter to her mom.

I didn't understand what Gracie was talking about at the time nor did I care.

Ramon was finished with his big bag full of dough. I could tell he was smiling through the handkerchief. He yelled, "Let's move!"

I tossed my bags over my shoulder and ran around the counter.

And there she was.

Little Gracie.

On her knees, hands folded, and eyes closed.

Whispering holy words. Praying to Jesus to protect me.

But it was too late. I didn't see her in time. The barrel of my .45 cracked her in the face. She fell to the ground unconscious. I shattered her nose. Blood poured everywhere.

Her mother screamed, "NO! NO! NO!"

She cradled Gracie. I took the handkerchief off my face and gave it to Gracie's mom to help stop the bleeding. She did the best she could. She looked up at me with tears in her eyes.

"Run. For the rest of your life. Leave and never come back...I'm... I'm so sorry."

She turned and tended to Gracie.

Ramon unlocked the door and we bolted down the street. We made it to the getaway car and drove slowly out of the alley. No one saw us. Ramon drove steadily and blended into traffic. The coppers drove past us towards the bank about five blocks out. We laughed.

I thought about Gracie's mom. I broke her daughter's nose, and she apologized to me? She seemed so concerned. What was that all about? Told me to run? Gracie praying because her dad was 'mean'?

Fuck that and fuck him.

I'd been in too many fights to count. One hit from me and he'd fold like a cheap suit.

I laughed again. We made it. We were headed up to Henry's apartment to split up the dough.

That's the last full memory I have of that day. Everything else is a blur. Bits and pieces.

I wasn't sure when I was taken, but it was either that night or the next morning.

I woke up on my back in a puddle. I looked around. It was dark. I was in a back alley next to a dumpster. All I could smell was blood and rotting garbage. My hands and feet were tied with rope. I tried to wiggle out. The knots were tight. I could barely see out of my right eye. My body was bruised all over. And I had a few busted ribs. Someone had worked me over pretty good. Everything hurt.

It felt like a dream, but this was my reality.

Headlights turned on in the alley from the left. I shuffled as hard as I could and sat up against the brick wall. I turned to avoid the light.

Ramon was sitting next to me. His hands and feet were also tied. I called out to him the best I could. My voice was a little more than a whisper.

Ramon? What the fuck? Ramon? Oh god. Oh fuck, Ramon. Talk to me, buddy.

As my eyes adjusted from the dark to the light I realized he was dead. Two big holes in his chest. I looked down. I was covered in blood. Most of it not mine.

As I said, I woke up in a puddle.

I was terrified. I began to quietly cry. Little Gracie's words echoed in my mind.

I don't need to pray for me. I need to pray for you.

I heard him get out of the car.

I'm scared for you.

The car door closed. I looked over. A silhouette of a giant.

Because daddy is mean.

He squatted down in front of me. He had a double barrel sawed-off shotgun in his right hand. He poked me in the head. I tried to hold my arms up in protest.

"You awake now, asshole? Fucking look up at me. Look up. Huh?"

His voice was deep. Gruff. I could smell the alcohol not only from his breath, but his whole being. He poked me in the head again. Ouch. He lit a cigarette.

"Just so you don't feel too bad, your friend over here is a fucking rat. Gave you up like Halloween candy when I showed up to his spot. You're a tough cookie though, I'll give you that. Thought I broke my fuckin' hand on your face. Comes with age, I guess. It ain't the old days, you know what I mean?"

He chuckled.

I didn't.

He took a long drag from the cigarette. He exhaled. Menthol. Yuck. Offered it to me. Before I replied he stuck it in my mouth.

"Everyone deserves a last smoke, even a faggot like you."

He shook his head.

"So let me get this straight. You fuckheads go into a bank and you're gonna rob the joint. That's fine. I don't care what you do in your spare time. But I'm trying to figure this out, here. You and your rat faggot pal here decide that it's okay to wave some guns at my wife and daughter, is that right? What is this? Fucking amateur night at the Apollo? Not only that, you pistol whip my daughter, and break her fucking nose? She's all kinds of fucked up now. Gonna have to get like three surgeries at least to get her nose *somewhat* back to normal. I got to go to the hospital and deal with these jack-off doctors to make sure she's taken care of. Are you out of your mind?"

I muttered the word 'accident'.

"You dumb motherfucker. Oh, it was an *accident*. Do I look like I give a shit about an accident? The damage is done. Cause and effect. That's why we're here. My wife... fucking unbelievable... actually asked me to spare you. Can you believe that? My own wife. The fuck is the world coming to? Said she saw your face. Said you looked genuinely sorry."

He poked me in the forehead again.

"Well guess what, asshole, I don't give a fuck how sorry you think you are. Faggot."

He stood up. I closed my eyes.

He shot me in each leg. In each shin.

Boom-Boom.

Point blank. It happened so fast.

He left me in the alley to bleed out. Slowly walked back to his car, in no particular rush, and backed out of the alley.

A couple walking their dog heard the gunshots and my screaming. I screamed not for help, but for a quick death which never came.

The ambulance showed up just in time.

They saved my life, but not my legs.

I wish Gracie had prayed harder.

Chapter 1,

Gracie

Dad had a brand new Lincoln. Black. Big V-8 engine. His pride and joy. Always washed it and kept the interior immaculate. He always checked my shoes before I got in to make sure they weren't dirty.

He wore the same outfit every day. It didn't matter if he was going to church or mowing the lawn. He had a stack of the same white long sleeve button-down shirts and navy blue dress pants. Black belt. Black dress shoes. Hair slicked back. Pack of smokes in his breast pocket. The only part of his outfit that changed every few days was his sport jacket. He had a few older, out of style tweed jackets with the leather elbow patches. I think they were from the seventies. Not sure why he liked them so much.

And he carried a gun. An old revolver. He always tried to hide it from me but I knew at a very young age that he was packing. He had an ankle holster for it. Never left the house without it. All vacations (which were not that many) were road trips. He refused to fly on planes.

I knew he went out drinking the night before.

He was drunk every night. He'd down at least a six-pack in the basement and *then* go out to the bar with the idea that if he showed up slightly faded he would drink less and spend less money.

False.

He'd close the bar down no matter what, whether he showed up there sober or shit-housed. When he came back to the house in the early AM he and mother would yell and scream. Sometimes they broke things. Sometimes he wouldn't come home at all. But when he did eventually turn up a few days later all hell would break loose. Wash, rinse, repeat.

Mother was furious. She threatened to leave so many times, but I knew she wouldn't. Mother lived for the church. Nothing was more important to her than preserving the *image* of her having a perfect family life, including her own safety.

Dad told Mother not to worry; he could stop drinking any time.

Yeah, right.

When I was ten, they started sleeping in different rooms. Other than fighting they barely spoke. They were *less* than roommates. No one on the outside knew this or even suspected anything was wrong. Our families on both sides knew for a fact that my parents had the strongest marriage ever. And at church every Sunday it was all hand-shakes and smiles.

All bullshit.

All lies.

He told me to get in the car. I went outside and waited for him to check if my shoes were acceptable for the journey. He checked. I got in. Put my seat belt on. Dad not so gracefully fell into the driver's

12

seat of the car and slammed the door a little too hard. He always slammed the door too hard while he was hungover. I jumped a bit, startled. I jumped every time he did it even though I knew it was going to happen. He put his head down and closed his eyes. Breathed slow, but intense. He had a full head of gray hair and one of those big veiny noses alcoholics get. Dad looked an easy ten years older than he was. High blood pressure, cholesterol, borderline diabetes. He was always sweating and wiping his brow, like he just ran five miles when all he did was walk down the driveway and get in the car.

"How you doing, Grace? We're gonna go for a ride, spend some dad-daughter time today, okay? Gotta talk to some people for a bit later on. You just sit there and behave, you got it? Then we'll, uh, get lunch or something."

Sit there and behave. Like I was a small child. And he always called me Grace. Everyone else on the planet called me Gracie. Because my name is Gracie.

"You know, I had to work for everything I got. Nothing was given to me. I grab life by the balls; squeeze and twist. Squeeze and twist, you catch that?"

He would always ramble this shit during a hangover. Which was every damn day.

"You know, sweetheart, I got a story I don't think you ever heard before. And I think you're old enough now to hear this. Some serious shit here. Listen up, kid."

Which meant one thing: some Army story I had heard at least a hundred times.

Probably about Afghanistan.

Probably about him and Chris.

Probably about him getting stabbed.

Probably about how many people he killed while in the service.

Probably about how the war was all bullshit.

Probably.

"So all this shit is going down, and it's going down bad. Me and Chris get separated from the unit, see. It was windier than shit and in the middle of all the chaos of gunfire and bombs it got silent. No wind, no sand, no bombs, no guns, no nothing. Chris and I turn a corner in an alley and there he is. He's just a kid, and he's got this fucking big ass kitchen steak knife. I'll be honest; I hesitated, for a fraction of a second. Me. Hesitate. Can you believe it? I don't give a shit about anybody, except you and ma, you know.

"The motherfucker stabs me twice. Happened so fast. Out of nowhere. Once in the leg, and once in the side of my gut. So Chris shoots the fucker, right? But it was this weird shooting, you know, where you'd think the blood is going to come out the other side and make a mess or something? But it doesn't. I don't know why. Usually point-blank shots are nasty. Usually.

"But we were low on ammo. We were surrounded, at least I thought we were. The fucking cowards were in the process of retreating, actually. Chris only shot him twice, but he wasn't dead yet. He was screaming and wiggling around in the fucking dirt. We didn't want anyone to hear this cocksucker, so Chris caves his melon in with the butt of his gun. Took him five hits to make the fucker stop moving. Fucker had a will to live. What a mess. But we had to put him out of his misery, you know? It was the *humane* thing to do. He was going to die anyways. And like I said, we were low on ammo. What are you gonna do? We were in the shit of it, you know?

"And I'll tell you something else. Your stomach muscles? Ain't no fucking joke. Ain't like the movies where some fucking jack-off gets shot or stabbed in the gut and still can crawl or walk. I dropped hard. Didn't even feel the leg wound, even though later I was told that was the worse of the two stabs."

Dad turned the key, backed out of the driveway, awkwardly straightened out the wheel, and put the gear lever into drive. I remember all the details of that day except for where we were going. I guess that's because we never made it there, wherever *there* was. We drove on and he continued with his blabbering.

"And all those ideas about God, duty, and patriotism? All gone in a second. The *pain*. Fuck. Couldn't believe it. Grew up as a good All American Christian boy my whole life and in that moment, in one fucking instant, to get rid of the hurt, I swear I would have sold my soul to the cheapest bidder, devil included.

"You know they train you to kill. Reset and train your mind to kill and move on. Those aren't humans over there, just targets. And really, they weren't people. You should see how these *people* live. See, some people like me don't need the mental training to learn how to kill and move on. It's just there. So when it happens the mind processes it like it's no big deal. Maybe natural, but probably because of how I grew up. Seeing the things I saw and doing the things I did, you know, in the old neighborhood. Now I did grow up seeing some terrible shit, shit you can't imagine. Shit I don't want you to imagine. Maybe not as bad as I seen in the war, but just as evil. At home it was real. Like a presence, a fog maybe is the best way to describe it. You got to live in it. But it shaped and molded me for what was to come. Get it?

"Over there it was just a job. And that's what I'm trying to keep you away from. I give you shit all the time about how good you have it, but in reality, I don't want you to end up like me. Understand, Grace?"

He looked over at me. I could smell the alcohol on his breath. I nodded in agreement.

"Now, anytime anyone finds out I was overseas, they say shit like, 'Thank you for your service,' and then want to shake my hand. Service of what? All the assholes I shot were uneducated little boys. If any of them were over twenty I'd be surprised. All of them were illiterate fucks, scared out of their minds, no combat training, trying to fight the greatest army in the history of the world. These fuckers were out there throwing rocks at tanks. No clue what was going on. The fucking president was always talking about spreading democracy and freedom and rights and all this shit. Get his fan base all riled up. Get votes. Stay in power. None of it real. None of it. These people don't want democracy; don't want it and don't need it. Don't understand it. Don't care about it. They couldn't figure out democracy from their dick in the fucking dirt. They're on a different level. And not a good level.

"So a few weeks before I was stabbed we were on patrol about forty klicks outside of Kabul. We go to this small village and the translator is talking to some of the goat herders. I mean these people are in bad shape physically. They're old and die at 45 years old if they make it that long. Our translator tells us not only do these people in the village not understand the concept of a 'unified Afghanistan', they don't even know about Kabul, what it is, and where it's at. *Kabul*, you know, the biggest city in all of Afghanistan, and it's twenty-five miles or so away. These people live and die in these small villages, never leaving other than going a few miles maybe to herd the goats and gather food and get buckets of water. No plumbing, no electricity.

There's no understanding of free-market enterprise or wanting/ needing to be a part of a government that represents the people. These are essentially... nomadic tribesmen and their only goal is to make it from one day to the next.

"Listen, there's nothing noble about war. It's all a glorified game of cowboys and Indians. I had thirteen confirmed kills. Thirteen is unlucky. Probably why I got stabbed. That might seem like a lot, but think about this. I was in-country for two hundred twenty days total. Those thirteen kills happened in nine combat situations. That means for two hundred plus days I was walking around the desert and the hills with my pud in my hands doing fuck all. But always ready, you know what I mean?"

I nodded. I had no clue what he was talking about or where this conversation was going. The reason I remember this day so well is because it was the first time I saw a dead body. Dad killed him.

Well, kind of.

He finally stopped talking. I thanked God.

We drove for a while and I dazed out the window, looking toward the river. I saw barges and boats in the distance. Wondered what it would be like to be a boat captain. We crossed the bridge and ended up going into a rougher part of the city on the north side. The old factories were all abandoned, windows were boarded up, graffiti sprayed everywhere. Some were cool murals, but most were gang tags or obscenities. Dad usually avoided this part of town. It was cold out, but Dad had his window down possibly hoping the cold air would help sober him up.

At a stoplight, a black man crossed the street and was coming towards us. Dad usually would have seen this coming and roll up the window up if he wasn't still faded from the night before.

The man put his arm through the window. Told Dad to get the fuck out. Dad looked up. The man had a gun. Dad always said he'd rather die than bow down to a nigger.

His words, not mine.

I never said my dad was a good guy, or even had any redeemable qualities. Sure he loved me in his own way I guess. Most people thought he was a good man, but that was just his public persona.

Yes, he served his country.

Yes, he went to church every Sunday.

Yes, he went to all my events.

Yes, he cared about my education.

Yes, he worked hard and paid the bills.

That all sounds good until you find out years later that the FBI had him linked to over thirty murders over a twelve-year period. But since he's dead now and the organization has been wiped out, we'll never know for sure.

Of all the cars in this city, this unlucky carjacker picked my dad's Lincoln. My chest tightened up, eyes teared up. The tension. I couldn't move. I could smell him, though. He was drunk, too. Dad very slowly grabbed the door latch with his left hand, put his right hand up in a surrendering motion.

"Take it easy, fella. We're getting out. You take the car. Take the money. Take it, we're not going to be any trouble."

He told Dad to not make any sudden mov-

Dad body checked the door as hard as he could. The gun went off. The bullet went through the roof.

"Goddamn! My fucking car!"

On the other side of the road the light was green. The gunman stumbled back across the median into oncoming traffic. He was clipped by a Buick. The Buick's driver didn't even have a chance to slow down. The impact from the car didn't kill him, but when his head hit the ground at an odd angle his neck snapped. His body twisted and contorted as it slid on the asphalt.

Dad looked at me and smiled. "Ha! Did you see that? What an asshole! I fucking swear to god, Grace. Every time I come up here it's something. FUCK!"

I was still shaking. The whole ordeal took maybe seven seconds. I was crying. Looking at the sunlight coming through the hole in the roof. Dad leaned over to my side of the seat. Tapped me on the cheek a few times.

"Gracie, You there? Calm down, baby, It's okay. Listen, listen, listen. This is very important okay? This is one of those times where I need you to man the fuck up, understand?"

I tried to stop crying.

It wasn't working.

"Gracie, listen. He. Is. Gone. And that's that. No two ways about it, get it? Look, these things happen more often than you think. He woke up today just like you and me. He decided to make poor choices, and now he's gone. That's it, end of story. Him or us. That's the way of the world. The motherfucker almost killed you. Thank god that car was coming the other way. I would have had to shoot him in broad daylight. Jesus. The fuck is this world coming to?"

He kissed me on the forehead and got out of the car. He walked over to the Buick. The elderly couple sat inside shocked. A few people ran over to the body. The old man began to get out of the driver's side. His wife stayed inside completely in shock.

The old man was shaking. Explained that he didn't even see him. He just came out of nowhere. Didn't have time to hit the brakes.

The old man's wife unbuckled her seat belt, but didn't get out. Dad smiled at her.

"Hey, don't worry about it lady. He was trying to carjack me. Pulled a gun and shot at my kid. If anything, she's the victim in all this. Fuck him."

Dad put his hand gently on the old man's shoulder.

"You did the world a favor, pops."

Four or five people were standing over the body. One lady was crying on her phone. She was on the line with the police. Dad and the old man walked over to the body. The old man squatted down and reached over to try and find a pulse. The old man's eyes welled up. He told the people in the circle that the carjacker was dead.

"No shit, pops. And don't cry over this fucking parasite, okay?"

The old man was having none of it. He was furious at Dad. Stood up and pointed his finger right in Dad's face. Asked him how he could have no compassion. Explained to him that this was a human life. And now it's gone because of their actions. How this young man was someone's son, someone's brother, maybe someone's father, mayb-

"Fuck you, Grandpa. See this?"

Dad walked over to the median and picked up the carjacker's gun. He walked back over to the old man and dangled the gun in front of his face.

"See this, you fucking prick? He pointed this at me. And honestly, I don't give a shit about that. I've had guns pointed at me before. So what? But... he pointed this at my daughter. That I will not accept. I don't give two fucks about him or his trash family. And don't you ever point your little finger in my face. I will fucking pistol whip you so hard your fat fucking cunt wife will have to feed you through a straw the rest of your goddamn life."

The old man backed down from dad.

Most men did.

Sirens were in the distance. Traffic was getting backed up. Cars passed slowly to look at the body. The old man asked Dad what they should do when the cops come.

"Easy, pops. No big deal. With cops, There's only one thing you gotta tell them."

He gave the old man a shit-eating grin.

"The truth."

Chapter 2,

Randy

I witnessed a murder when I was twenty-two.

In the old days, weed was illegal in our state. Not like today, where you can just pop in to any shop on any block and purchase the best hash money can buy. You had to deal with the local weed man. Usually he was some saggy pants neck tattoo asshat that drove a lowered Honda with a bolt-on wing. He'd usually overcharge but would always promise his next shipment would be 'the shiz-nit'. The situation sucked but that's just the way it was in the old days.

So one day I called up my hookup, Steffan, to see if he could deliver a dime bag of that sticky ick green green over at the gas station. It was around noon and my shift was over at four that day. It was so slow so getting high as Mt. Everest on the devil's lettuce wouldn't be that big of a deal.

Steffan pulled up about an hour later. I didn't see him, but I could hear his shitty rice burner muffler out in front of the building.

He did have a good sound system, though. I could hear the bass beats as they mildly resonated through the building.

I asked Marta, the other gal there, to watch the register while I went on break. She rolled her eyes. She knew who Steffan was. She knew why I was going on break.

Steffan and I walked out to the back dumpster. I give him some dough and he gave me a small bag of that sticky ick green green. Looked like better quality than usual. Smelled like heaven.

I loaded my pipe.

Flicked my Bic.

Breathed in.

Felt the smoke slowly fill my lungs.

Closed my eyes.

Held it in for as long as I could.

Oh fuck.

Fuck me.

This was a little stronger than what I was used to.

I choked.

Coughed.

A lot.

When I get that really good shit I can't move all that much. Time slows. I took another hit. Smiled. Felt my eyelids close. Like *really* felt them move over the membrane of my eyeballs. At this point I was floating. I grabbed a handle on the dumpster because I was worried about falling off of the planet.

I passed the pipe to Steffan. He took two hits. We stared at each other in silence just appreciating the moment. He broke the silence. Said my eyes were as red as the devil's dick. I would have laughed if I could move my face.

What happened next I can but at the same time can't recall.

Behind the gas station there was an apartment complex being built. Being as it was a Sunday, no workers were there. Out of nowhere, these two guys are chasing each other through the construction zone. The first man was very chubby and slow. He wasn't going to make it that far. He was yelling 'please' and 'no' as he tried to get away. The second man caught up to him pretty quick. He was a massive force. Big guy. Must have been six foot six. Maybe taller. He was older. Had the nicest suit on.

I tried to ask Steffan where in the fuck these guys came from. He had his eyes closed. Smiling. Stuck in a different dimension, apparently. He opened his eyes and laughed. And then to our horror, we realized they were fighting to the death.

Steffan and I were in no position to do anything about the situation. We couldn't call the cops, couldn't break up the brawl, and couldn't run away. As usual we were as high as a Chinese bamboo kite and about as useful as tits on a bull. Steffan slowly grabbed my hand. He squeezed gently. I squeezed back. It was all the movement we had.

The chubby man was stabbed a few times and at that point they were both on the ground wrestling for the knife.

Hitting.

Slapping.

Choking.

Biting.

Kicking.

The chubby man tried to get up but was shoved hard into a pile of bricks. Most of them fell over. I couldn't hear what he was saying, but I knew he was pleading for his life. The big man stood over him. He didn't have the knife. He didn't need it.

Steffan somehow sobered up enough to run away. Hopped in his car and peeled out of the parking lot. Up and left me out back sixty feet away from a dead fat man and a giant psychopath. I walked back inside when I could feel my legs again.

Marta went outside to take the trash out about twenty minutes after the incident and 'found' the body. She ran in the gas station crying and screaming. I called 911. I comforted Marta until her husband showed up and took her home. We didn't have working security cameras at the gas station(thank god) so when I was questioned by the police I pretended to be completely shocked. The last thing I needed was a giant hitman mobster-looking motherfucker coming after me.

I read in the papers the next day that the fat man's name was Henry. He owned a bar called Smiley's in a shadier part of town. Must have gotten mixed up with the wrong people.

Steffan and I made an agreement to never talk to anyone about what we had seen. The big man saw us for sure. I remember thinking he looked familiar, but like I said, everything was so hazy. And I was scared out of my mind.

Chapter 3,

Robbie

Me and Paw Paw went down to the fishing hole on a Sunday morning. I was eight or nine at the time.

He had these fence poles and a tarp he used as a makeshift tent. Some contraption he made in his spare time. It folded up and fit perfectly in the backseat of his car. He'd also bring these old wooden folding chairs. I swear I'll never find anything that comfy again.

The other kids in the project never wanted to go, but Paw Paw would still invite them. Guess they were scared of him.

I always liked to go. Nice change of scenery. I liked the car ride, too. Way better than sitting on the bus.

I stayed with Paw Paw a lot. Dad was dead (at least that's what I was always told) and Mom was always trying to find a fix. Back then Mom would have strangers stay the night and kick me out. Paw Paw let me stay on his couch. I'd sleep with his cat, Blueberry.

So that particular Sunday we loaded up the fencepost tent and fishing rods up in the back of his old beat-up Ford Falcon. That old car was beat to hell and smoked more than a chimney. Always had at least one donut on it.

He forgot the tackle box. Asked me to go on inside and get it. I ran inside, grabbed it, put it in the trunk, and off we went. Along the way we stopped and picked up a sack of burgers for lunch. Such a perfect day. Nothing could mess it up. I remember riding in the Falcon with the windows down without a care in the world. Like I was free.

After a few minutes, I realized we weren't going the right way. I asked where we were going. Paw Paw told me about a new lake out west of town he wanted to try out. The papers said it was recently stocked with catfish, and plenty of them. Paw Paw was really good with the reading. He read the paper every day. He even knew how to read books. Most of them in the project couldn't read a damn street sign. Paw Paw read better than anyone I knew.

We ended up at the most beautiful lake I'd ever seen. On one side there was a golf course. I'd never seen a golf course before other than on the TV. Grass greener than St. Patrick's Day. On the other side, the most beautiful houses ever. I asked Paw Paw if people really lived in them houses. He said of course they do.

None of the kids in the project would believe me if I told them about this place.

We parked the car and walked a ways with our gear over a hill and found the perfect spot by a few trees. The shade went over the water, which was good. Fish circulate in cool water when it's really hot outside. I ate a burger while Paw Paw set up the tent and chairs.

We forgot the tackle box. Again. I asked Paw Paw for the keys and headed back to the car. I opened the trunk only to realize I grabbed a small toolbox instead of the tackle box back at Paw Paw's place. Oops. I ran back to Paw Paw to tell him my mistake. He told me not to worry about it. Almost everything he needed was on the poles, and the bait was in a separate bag. All he needed was some weight for the fishing line. He told me to grab the toolbox. Maybe there was something small inside he could use to weigh the line down.

I went back to the car again. I went around to the trunk and a white man was standing there. His hand was leaning on the trunk. He was tall, with a flannel shirt, jeans, and cowboy boots. He had long blond hair and a bushy beard. He smiled at me. His teeth were yellow and stained.

"What you doin' up here, boy?"

I told him me and Paw Paw were going fishing.

"Really? Is that so. Is that your papa over there?" He pointed at Paw Paw.

I told him he ain't my daddy. Paw Paw is his name. We don't want no trouble, mister. I told him Paw Paw read in the paper there's some good catfish in this lake. We were going to have a cookout back at the project. It's smelly when you gut them, but the nuggets turn out delicious. Paw Paw's secret recipe.

"Is that so?" He smiled at me again. Creepy fucker.

I walked away and back to Paw Paw with the toolbox. I told him about the white man. Told him the white man made me feel uneasy. Paw Paw didn't seem concerned. We were just there to fish. If he wants to come back and cause trouble, well, that was his problem. He told me people been pushing him around his whole life. Why would today be any different?

He looked through the toolbox. The smallest piece was a large spark plug. A lot bigger than what he needed, but it would do the job.

He tied the plug to the line and cast it in the water not too far from the shore.

We waited. Paw Paw said we shouldn't have to wait too long. We were using a chopped up beef liver for bait. Stunk to high heaven, but always worked at the old fishing hole. We dug into the rest of the burgers. I opened a cola. Paw Paw cracked open a cold one. The weather was perfect. Still no bites.

"Hey there! Uh-huh, hey you!"

We looked behind us. There he was, walking toward us. The tall white man by the car.

"My name's Lee Ritz, and you got me all kinds of fired up! You!"

When he said 'you' he was pointing at Paw Paw.

"What are you doin' here, boy?"

I wondered why he would call Paw Paw 'boy'. Paw Paw was an old man. Grey hair and everything. He was at least fifty years old. Older than Mr. Lee Ritz for sure.

Paw Paw kept his cool. He explained we were just there to fish. Minding our own business. Also, there weren't any 'No Colored' signs posted by the lake.

"Are you kidding me? Project Niggers. Here. Fishin' on my golf course lake. In this part of town we don't need no goddamned signs. I'll tell you what, this here world is going to hell in a handbasket. You got some fuckin' stones on you nigger for coming up here. Now pack your shit and get. The. Fuck. Out."

He pointed at the car. He raised his voice.

"Now, Niggers! I ain't got all fuckin' day!"

Now I was scared out of my mind. Paw Paw sighed. I saw a flash of anger in his eyes, but he still kept cool.

I wasn't scared of this Lee Ritz character.

I wasn't scared because we were out of the project.

I wasn't scared because this guy was at least a foot taller than Paw Paw.

I was scared because I didn't know what Paw Paw was going to do. See, Paw Paw was old school. A real gangster from the old days. Fought in the streets against the Italians.

And that ain't no joke.

When the Italians wanted you dead, you died. Simple as that. But Paw Paw survived time after time. I've seen him down at the dumpster taking out the trash without a shirt on. I've never seen so many scars.

Bullet holes.

Cuts.

Burns.

Lashes.

We all heard the stories.

How he crawled four city blocks with three bullets in his gut.

How he was missing a few toes on his right foot after a pipe bomb explosion at a late-night poker game.

How when he was in prison he spent more time in the infirmary than in a cell because he kept getting stabbed.

I don't know where the burn scars came from, but there were plenty.

Paw Paw always said nobody is lucky. People go when their time is up. Ain't no two ways 'bout it. They called him Paw Paw not because he was someone's daddy, but because he had the biggest hands anyone had ever seen. And he fought to the death. He was the animal. The beast.

Paw Paw asked Lee again to leave us alone. All we want to do is some fishin'. Please leave us be.

"Are you serious? Get out of here! Pack your shit and leave now. You. Are. Not. Welcome. Here. What don't you understand? You got ten seconds to get your shit packed or I'm going up the block and getting the boys over at Sullivan's Place. You will be in a world of hurt. Your choice, nigger. What you want to do?"

Paw Paw reeled in the line. Leaned the fishing pole up against his chair. Lit a cigarette and took a long, cool drag. Told Lee to go over to wherever the fuck Sullivan's was and go get dem boys. Tell dem boys to come down by the lake. Let's dance, white boy.

"Your funeral! Idiot!"

Now I was terrified. How many would come back?

Lee turned to walk back up the hill. Paw Paw locked the line on the fishing pole. It wasn't fully reeled in; the spark plug was still hanging about five feet down. He followed Lee Ritz up the hill and swung the pole as hard as he could. Cracked Mr. Lee Ritz right on top of the head.

Lee took maybe ten uneven steps, each slower than the last. He was so disoriented he couldn't walk straight. His hands couldn't reach his head. He twitched as he tried to regain his balance. Paw Paw still had the line locked on the pole. He ran over and cracked him in the head again. Swung with both hands over his head straight down. Crack. Like a ripe melon falling on the curb.

Lee Ritz dropped. Hard.

Paw Paw came back over and started to disassemble the tent. I helped. We gathered the gear and put it in the car. It took us two trips. We didn't go fast.

Paw Paw told me that the world's a hard place. You can be pushed around or push back. It's that simple.

The difference between Lee and Paw Paw is that Lee *thought* he was a tough guy.

Paw Paw *was* a tough guy.

Before we left I asked Paw Paw what we should do. Was he dead? Paw Paw said he wasn't dead. It wasn't a big deal. Just another white man sleeping in the grass.

We didn't have a fish fry that night.

Chapter 4,

Gracie

So my nose is still crooked from getting hit during that bank heist all those years ago. I don't remember much from it. Mother always said I was fearless. Everyone terrified while I stood up and talked back to the robbers. She always said I got my fearlessness from dad.

I've had a few plastic surgeries, but at this point I was finished seeing doctors. Dad, for the first time in his life, actually agreed with me on something. He hated seeing me in the hospital. Pissed him off.

It was almost seven years since my nose had been broken. Or as Dad always said, completely fuckin' shattered.

So at the beginning of high school we moved. The new house we moved into was so much bigger, and on a quiet street. It was weird being out of the city in a place so calm. Mother loved the new house. The yard had a section laid out for a garden so Mom could finally plant the fruits and vegetables she had always wanted to grow and pick. The kitchen was recently updated with all new appliances and had a giant island. As for myself I had a big room upstairs complete with a balcony. Dad had the basement. A 'man cave'. An office, nice leather chairs, a pool table, a bar.

He held meetings down there in the basement with the guys he worked with. I always knew Dad worked long hours and provided for us, but even then in high school I didn't really understand (or care) that what he did for a living was well, questionable, to say the least.

Dad was a gangster. I don't really know the hierarchy of where he was in the mob, but he was more than a typical hoodlum. I know now that he killed people. Lots of people. And was good at it. He came back from the service and found a job with a logistics company through family connections. Mother said he was on his way to the top. We were set up for life. Great pay, good hours, perfect benefits, and lots of vacation time.

He threw it all away to work for Mr. Kearsey.

And I'll never *really* know why. Although, I do have a theory.

Mother's theory involves the military. While Dad was in the service, he was respected. Soldiers have a brotherhood. Camaraderie. Bonds that can't be broken. She says Dad would do anything to have that back. Even if that meant giving his life to those animals, as she called them.

My theory? He enjoyed killing people. He liked getting away with it. He relished the fact that everyone knew what he did, and sometimes knew who he killed. He loved knowing no one would rat on him or they would be next.

He loved the money.

The girlfriends.

The drugs.

The power.

When you live with people long enough, you know there's some things about them that they never show the outside world. Some things stay in their hearts behind closed doors, yet define their being at all times.

In a way, Dad was more powerful than Mr. Kearsey.

Yes Mr. Kearsey was the boss and he had the money and had a solid crew. But Mr. Kearsey never did any of the dirty work. At least not anymore. He was always at the lounge in the basement with the old-timers planning and making more of the 'big picture' decisions. Of course Dad sat in on a lot of these meetings. Helped make moves on other gangs, figure out scores, etc.

I couldn't fully grasp any of this as a child, but I knew he was different from the other dads I went to school with.

I wasn't allowed in the basement. Any time I went down there Dad got mad. Furious. So of course I would sneak down there from time to time.

Noise.

Shit.

DAD.

And someone else.

I was in the basement. I should have run upstairs; there was a chance I would have not been seen coming up. But, if I was caught, there would be hell to pay. If Dad found out I was hiding down there, he'd kill me.

There was a small space under the bar. I crawled in and curled myself into a ball. Breathed quiet as humanly possible. I heard them coming down the stairs.

Shit.

It was Dad and Sal. Sal was another person employed by Mr. Kearsey. Sal was the boss' right-hand man. The consigliere of the organization. And he was fat. Like, really fat. And he moved his arms the wrong way when he walked. When he walked forward he looked like he was going backwards. Almost made you dizzy. Took him two minutes to walk down the steps. Each step groaned as he walked down. One step at a time. Both feet on each step. I once saw him wipe his brow after picking up a pencil.

Sal sat down with a loud thud on a couch about ten feet away from me. Dad was pacing impatiently.

I waited.

Listened.

Couldn't believe my ears.

"What's going on, Sal? Why are you really here? I know you're not here to check out the house, and my wife fucking hates you and you hate her. So what gives?"

"Well, I got some bad news. You hear about Nick?"

"Nick who? Which Nick? I know a thousand fucking Nicks, Sally. You'll have to be a little more specific."

"The boss' kid Nick. The kid, you know."

"Yeah? What about him?"

"He made a move. On his own."

"Fucking Christ Almighty."

"Yeah, yeah, It's bad. He's in hiding; the boss is gearing up for a possible war. It's as bad as it gets right now. You might want to sit down for this."

"Fuck you, you fat cunt."

"Excuse me? You don't talk to me like that, okay? You need to show some respec-"

"Sally, stop right now. You come in my fucking house, tell me some kid, some non made man, makes an unsanctioned hit against a rival, and now I gotta gear up and go to war? I have to take care of his shit? We've been at peace for five years. Five years this plan, that I helped set up, not you, has been working beautiful. Everyone stays in their territories, and everyone has their own businesses split up and everyone makes money. This whole fucking city is making money."

"I know, bu-"

"Apparently you don't know. Look around. Everyone is rich. WE. ARE. ALL. RICH. The new Caddy you drive is paid for. Your wife's Caddy is paid for. This house is paid for! This isn't the old days where we have flashy shit and it's all a facade, some bullshit all on credit and we're living score to score, job to job, like fucking street animals, man. This money, the shit we do now, the money makes itself. And our legit enterprises are going strong! Also, *because* our money is so good, and we don't do anything illegal much anymore, we don't recruit. We have no people for a war. Who did he fuck with? Maybe I can smooth this over. And don't you ever, ever fucking come in my house and tell me to sit down. This is my fucking house."

"He shot Paw Paw."

Dad paused. A loss for words. For the first time since he came out of the womb.

"Why? Why. We've been at peace with the niggers for five years. Tell me why, and it better be a good reason. This is beyond anything we can handle. Beyond anything we can clear up."

"Revenge. For killing the boss' brother all them years ago. The kid's uncle, you know, they were close. Kid's always held a grudge. I guess maybe he wanted to prove that he was one of us, you know."

"No. No, I don't know. What do you mean, revenge? For the last war? Ten...eleven fucking years ago? That's not how this works. These people know only one language. Violence. Hits are only to be sanctioned from above, and by above I mean higher than Christ himself."

"I know, I know."

"You keep saying that. *I know, I know.* Apparently, you know a lot, except for what to fucking do, which is I guess why you're here. Listen, and listen close to my words. You said he shot Paw Paw. Did he shoot him, or DID-HE-KILL-HIM? Those are two separate things, understand? Do we have confirmation on a dead body? Did anyone see him do it? If no one saw him and we got a dead body, we could be in the clear, could just be some nigger neighborhood vendetta. No big deal."

"Well, we know he was shot twice in the chest. With a .45."

"IS HE DEAD! IS HE FUCKING DEAD! DO WE HAVE A BODY! CAN YOU GIVE ME A STRAIGHT FUCKING ANSWER?!"

"We don't have a body, but no one, not even Paw Paw could take a hit like that. Not at his age. He's got to be in his sixties by now."

"Are you listening to yourself? Are you listening to the words coming out of your fucking mouth? This guy took out four of our guys, including Mikey the Fighter, all who had guns, with a fucking straight razor in his boot. He's been hung from a tree. I poured gasoline on him once and lit him on fire. Do you understand who we are fucking dealing with? The man cannot die. Was Nick seen? Please tell me no."

"Someone saw his Camero. You know, that white and blue piece of shit with the loud exhaust?"

"Fuck. *Fuck.*"

I heard fear in Dad's voice. That was the year Dad was gone a lot and the news reports were filled daily with article after article about killings in the city. Most people blamed it on 'black on black' violence. Others on guns and lack of gun control laws.

After they left, I crawled out from under the bar. I spent the rest of the day with a pretty terrible leg cramp.

Chapter 5,

Frederick

So back in the day I found this job in town. It was over at that fancy-schmancy mall where all them uppity fuckers go to. My position, you ask? Security guard. I was a big shot, if you catch my drift. And they even paid me $8.50 an hour, thank you very much. Highest paying job I ever had. Looks like I was moving on up in the world. Liked to have seen someone try and stop me. Good luck to you, asshole.

I'd spend my days catching bad guys.

Thieves.

Loiterers.

Homeless.

Not on my watch, fuckers.

Guess you could say I was damn near a detective. Hell, with my uniform on and shield on my chest some people did think I was a cop. They'd straighten up as they walked by and call me 'sir'.

Goddamned right.

Come to think of it I pretty much *was* a cop. I had to call them if situations got too out of control. Hell, I was the one doing all the dirty work. Then the boys in blue would show up and take all the credit. That's OK though. I knew they considered me one of their own. We had an understanding. I'm sure of it.

My biggest bust was over at Solomon's Electronics. Caught one of his employees (turned out to be the owner's nephew) puttin' some speakers in the trunk of his car after work one night. Turns out this fuckin' heeb had stolen over ten grand in merch over the last three years. Almost threw out my shoulder patting myself on the back after that sting operation, thank you very much.

Sometimes famous folk like to come up to the mall to go shopping. Their people will call ahead of time wanting a personal escort. Show 'em around and such. I was security after all, so naturally that person was me.

Been lifting weights at the house. Not real weights, that would be too expensive. Money don't grow on trees, see. I got a good system. I put rocks in milk jugs and walked around the block. One time I did three laps. Think about that. I was built like a brick shit house.

I also was a good fighter. Really good. One of the greats if you ask me.

Marty Jones once gave me shit. I knocked him clean the fuck out. I threw an old tire at him. Slapped him upside the head pretty good.

Night night, you dumb cunt.

His wife ran out of the trailer and threw a bottle at me. Said she'd sue me. I told her to stick that bottle where the sun don't shine, if you catch my drift.

Her butt. That's where the sun don't shine.

See, old Marty was out of line. He was a little bit drunk on the sauce again. Kept rambling on and on about how I'd never get into the Klan on account of my wife being a nigger and that my son was a half nigger. And that really hurt my feelings.

I still thought I could get in the Klan. I wasn't no nigger.

And yes, I did marry a colored gal. Fuck you, you judgmental prick. Pussy is pussy. It all feels the same in the dark. We've had sex at least ten times. Maybe eleven. I lost count a while ago.

Her family didn't take too kindly to me. And they sure as hell didn't like all of my confederate flags. I only had three. One hung up in the living room and the other two were on flagpoles on the back of my dodge pick up truck. God bless America.

Sometimes when I have too many Busch Light beers I'll take the flag off the living room wall and tie it around my neck as a makeshift cape. I'll walk around the trailer park yelling and ranting about how the south shall rise again. Which it will. We all know it.

I had to watch out, though. If I was out too long the wife would get mad. Sometimes she'd throw things at me. One time she got me good in the neck with a frying pan. Cast iron. Fuck. She'd hit me, I'd hit her. It's all good though. You got to keep the colored in line. It's the only way. Wasn't as bad as you'd think.

So on that day, I got the call. Mr. T was coming to the mall. Mr. T! Never met a movie star before. The most famous person I'd escorted was a State Senator. I was smarter than him. Probably could lift more, too. Maybe the politicians could give me a call. I sure got a lot of ideas.

Lady manager at the desk says I gotta take Ed with me when Mr. T shows up.

Fuck.

I hate Ed. Too nice to everyone. Smiled all the time. Wasn't interested in joining the Klan. What the hell did he have to live for, then? He was too young. I think he was 22 at the time. I was 47 at the time so I had the knowledge and experience to run this ship.

But whatever. At least he could help me with my plan.

I wanted to get a picture of Mr. T and myself shaking hands and someday give it to my half breed kid. My son would know that I was hip. That I once was a bodyguard for one of the toughest negroes in the business.

But I needed a camera. I went over to Solomon's Electronics. He wasn't there. His wife was though. Pretty good lookin' for a Jew broad.

Hey, there! Jew broad! I yelled as I walked in the shop. Had a big smile on my face. All in jest, you see. I'm cool with these people after I busted their nephew.

"Excuse me?"

She looked up.

"You can leave my store right now. Get out. Now."

She seemed firm. Angry. Like she didn't get my sense of humor.

You are of the Jewish faith, correct? You are a female, correct? I asked.

"Um, yes? Now get the hell out of my store!"

She seemed more agitated. Her voice was raised.

Then you're a Jew broad! I smiled from ear to ear. I had a pretty good smile. I was only missing two bottom teeth at the time.

"Get the fuck out of my store or I'm calling the cops!"

I was a bit confused. So I told her what was up. I am the cops! Idiot! I'm the one that saved your store from being robbed and all I want to do is spend my hard-earned American money here, but I guess I'll spend it elsewhere, thank you very much! Good day you dumb, idiot woman!

The customers froze and stared at me. I'm sure they all saw how stupid she was behaving.

I stormed out. Went over to the Walgreen's across the parking lot. Bought a camera. A nice one, too. Cost me over thirteen dollars, but that's okay because I'm all about quality.

So I went out to the entrance to meet Ed. He's there on time, as usual.

Show off.

I tell him the plan.

Okay Ed, now don't fuck this up. Mr. T. is showing up any minute. He'll be in a black limousine. When he steps out of the car I'm going to shake his hand. At that exact moment I'm going to look over at you and smile. When I smile all you have to do is aim the camera and hit the big red button on the top. Can you do that? It's not that fucking hard. It's not rocket science, see?

"Got it. No problem," Ed said.

The plan was perfect. Simple. My wife would think I'm a hero. I might even get to see her naked again.

The limo pulled up in the parking lot. Ed looked up at me.

"Hey Frederick."

Not now, Ed. Get the camera ready. No time for small talk right now you ass hat.

He looked at the camera. Confused.

"Well, it's just that I....."

Ed! For the love of God can you shut, shut, shut the fuck up! This is the most important moment of my life and you're blabbering on about fuck knows what. Always mumbling about this and that. Can you just do your job and hit the god damned red button?

Ed looked down. The limo pulled up to us. The door opened.

"Did you buy any film?"

Chapter 6,

Robbie

The North Side.

People avoid it like the plague. Cops don't patrol here anymore unless they get specifically called in and that's usually for dead bodies. There aren't even enough cops for the job. Not enough firemen. Not enough medical personnel. The water is dirty. No one wants to be here in this fucking war zone. There's no tax revenue, so no pensions for the cops, or the city workers for that matter. The government here is a revolving door, and it doesn't help that everyone riots every few years. Even the supermarkets are leaving. They can't find employees or managers, the customers and employees steal, and after a few years of running at a loss the corporate office forces them to shut it all down. So now we got to travel, most of us by bus, for food, to places that don't want us there. I see the looks on them old white faces when I use Mom's EBT card. The other option is surviving on canned goods from gas stations, but even those are getting further and further away. And schools? A complete joke. The teachers never last more than two years, no matter what incentives are tossed their way. Most of the kids go for the free breakfast and lunch. Our housing is government subsidized, so it's shit, too. Nothing is ever maintained or repaired. Every year there is another complex that is condemned and has to be boarded up. It's so bad we don't even have homeless people hanging around.

Our place is on its last legs. Hopefully lasts a few more years.

Heard a weak knock at the door.

What the fuck did he need now?

I was still up. It was around three AM. I knew who it was. This punk-ass bitch been comin' around here for years. Always something. Brother and I were alone now for four days. Or was it five? We was almost out of food. Still had some of that cereal left. No milk, though. Spread it out and it might last us two more days.

It was Ray Ray at the door, I was sure, Mom's boyfriend. A fucking low life pimp. Always hitting her, hitting me. Always hitting little brother. Always drunk. Always taking our money. Always high as fuck; a broke ass, food stamp stealing nigga. Always making Mom work. He'd string her out on the powder, always leaving her wanting more. To make more she had to work harder. She was gone for days at a time. I was older now. Didn't make me smarter, but I knew what was going on. Made her his slave. Whored her out to who the fuck ever over at the hotel a few blocks away. I heard for one hour you could do anything you want for two hundred. Anything. If the girls were younger it cost fifty more. For twenty-five more you can fuck without a condom. The money all went to Ray Ray first. The girls never touched it. Who knows what he paid them; probably close to dog shit. All that money went up his nose.

Ray Ray had five or six girls at any given time. Sometimes I met them. Some were nice. Some were close to my age. He'd beat all of them; they usually had to wear caked on makeup before taking any clients. Most of the girls disappeared after about three months. I'd like to think they escaped and maybe went home, if they had a home to go back to. Found a job. Or maybe one of the johns helped them escape the life. But that was all wishful thinking. These girls were all orphaned trash that were turned out of or ran away from the system. A system that's undermanned and underfunded to begin with. And the johns? Well, you don't go to Ray Ray if you're an upstanding member of the community. You go to Ray Ray if you want to tie up little girls. You go to Ray Ray if you have sick fetishes. Rumor was, one of the johns killed a girl once. Ray Ray charged the killer two hundred more dollars for the trouble of getting rid of the body.

So even though Mom made good money we never saw any of it. The only time Mom was here was maybe for a day at a time when she was too tired to work. I was left to take care of little brother myself. Little brother was half white. He didn't know who his daddy was. Nobody did. The other kids made fun of him. Always calling him half breed. He was six now. I was really hard on him when it came to behaving and discipline. Made sure to spank him or put him in the corner when he messed up, even for the tiniest infraction. The result was the most quiet and obedient little boy. People commented all the time when we were out in the neighborhood about how good he was. How quiet he was and how he never left my side. How he listened when I told him to come here, do this, do that.

I had to make sure he didn't fuck around. I knew child services would catch up to Mom sooner or later. They'd put us in foster care and probably split us up. I needed little brother to know his manners at the table. Not throw toys. Not lash out when he didn't get his way.

Mom was on the bad path. No fairy tale ending to her story. Close to the end, I hate to admit. Looking skinnier and weaker every time I saw her. Looked like she was losing hair, too.

But I was bigger now. Last time Ray Ray hit brother I almost hit back. I stood up, looked him in the eye. Face to face.

"Okay, okay, young nigga. I like that. Got a little fight in you now, huh? Fuck you gonna do? Wanna try and be a man up in this bitch? You ain't nothin', nigga. I'll smoke you anytime I want."

He slapped me in the head. Hard.

"You gonna hit back, young nigga? Do it. Please." He swayed in front of me. Smiled. Taunted.

I didn't move.

I wanted to.

Didn't.

Paw Paw always taught me to pick my battles. The hardest part is to not lash out. The hardest part is holding back, even when the enemy is most deserving. Paw Paw once told me-

If you fuck with someone dangerous make sure you can finish the job. If you fuck with someone real, someone hard, you gotta be prepared for retaliation. You gotta hit so hard they can't get back up. If they're still alive, make sure if they're ever about to pass you on the sidewalk and they see you they'll cross the street. Don't waste time on weak brothas. Most these niggas out here are all flash. All fancy chains and teeth. Big rims and speakers. Niggas can't even put on a belt talking about how they 'know people'. When someone says they 'know people', know this: That is a weak brotha.

If you don't kill, always wound. Always maim. Always scar. If he see that scar on his face every time he wash his face, he'll remember you. If he limp everywhere he go, with every step he'll remember your name. This is the world we live in. Not twenty miles away other youngsters your age live different lives. Live in nice houses in the burbs worried about a science project or a swim meet; this is not your world. They don't worry about food. Clothes. Shelter. Child Protective Services. Wondering if they'll have lights on or heat. Wondering if they'll have water. Wondering if some wannabe hard nigga gonna blast them for wearing the wrong color hat.

You have real problems. You know more pain and suffering right now than any of those fools will ever experience in their lives. Remember: That's what makes you stronger. That's what's going to pull you through anything. Knowing that you can take the heat and they can't.

I walked to the door of the apartment. Braced myself for whatever bullshit Ray Ray had on the other side. Closed my eyes. Exhaled. Turned the handle. Pulled.

Paw Paw fell in the door at my feet.

Blood.

All over him. All over the ground. Trailed all the way down white tiles in the hallway. I reached down and dragged him inside. Directly to my right I dragged him into the kitchen area. He was heavy. Dead weight. The blood under him made him easier to slide. I propped his back up against the stove.

"I called George."

Quiet, Paw Paw. Quiet, now. Don't move. Stay still. Shit.

"It's all good, my young friend. Just stay with me 'til George shows up. He'll know what to do. Get me back to normal in no time."

George was a fixer. A hustler with a small but tough crew. He went to medical school on a scholarship when he was young but didn't make it. Ended up moving back to the hood. He can patch you up if it ain't bad enough. You had a fifty-fifty chance when George showed up and you were wounded. He was good at getting rid of bodies, too. We can't go to the hospital after a shooting or a stabbing; they're required by law to report it. Then some detective gets involved asking questions, which leads to nowhere because no one will talk, and even if they did, these cops don't give a shit about solving crimes in this part of town.

What happened? What happened, Paw Paw, stay with me. Stay awake, come on. Just til George gets here.

Looks like he was shot at least twice. Once in the gut. Once in the shoulder. But there was more blood coming from somewhere else, I think.

He put pressure on the gut wound with his right hand. Held my hand with his left. Closed his eyes.

"Two white boys. Camero. White and blue. Blasted my ass. Aw fuck."

He stopped to breathe. Made a gurgling noise. Coughed weakly.

"Shot four, five times and peeled out. Fuck. I ain't done any jobs in years. Fuck they trying to take me out for. Fuck. Walked all the way here. Had to crawl up them steps to get here, though."

So you talked to George? He's on the way here? The fuck is taking him so long?

George only lived in the next building over. If Paw Paw called him when he got shot, George should have seen him come in or been here already.

"Yeah I talked to him. He'll be here soon. He's patching up Big Dil right now. He got stabbed yesterday."

Everyone getting shot or stabbed. I couldn't wait to get out of this godforsaken place.

I heard the doorknob turn, thank God. Finally. George. I popped my head out from around the stove. My second disappointment for the night.

Ray Ray.

Fuck.

"Fuck all this blood up in here? Who da fuck is bleedin'? That you, young nigga? What you do, mess with the wrong bull?"

We need help; we're waiting for George.

"Shit, who knows when he's gonna be here. Heard that nigga Big Dil got stabbed by some punk-ass negroes. You know George over there fixin' his ass up. Big fuckin' Dil done ran his mouth too many times."

Ray Ray turned the corner. Smiled when he saw us.

"Well, well. Hey there, Paw Paw! The fuck happened to you? Heard some white boys popped someone 'bout half an hour ago. Wouldn't think it'd be you. Who'd you piss off this time; I thought you was out the game, my nigga."

"I ain't yo nigga."

"Fuck you then. I ain't got time for no dyin' old ass man. Robbie, look up here."

I looked up. He was high and drunk. Didn't care that a man was dying right in front of him.

"Need that money you got save up for that phone you was gettin'. I'll pay you back nigga, you know I good for it."

No.

"Fuck you say to me, boy?"

No. Get out of here. Help me or get. I gotta stop this bleedin'. He's dying, here.

Paw Paw closed his eyes. *Fuck. Wake up, buddy.*

"Nigga, I done told you I need that money. I know you got at least thirty dollas up in here and you gonna give it up. Now, you stupid fuck. Give it up! Before I whoop dat ass, nigga."

No.

"No? Oh really, now?"

He hit me. Close fist-ed.

Paw Paw opened his eyes. Spoke weakly, "No, don't do it. Don't do it... no. He ain't worth it. Don't kill him."

I stood up. Ray Ray squatted down.

"I'll do whatever the fuck I want, you old bag. I run this shit. I don't care if you on your deathbed or not; repeat, I RUN THIS SHIT. Me. I'm king dick in this bitch, motherfucker. Tell me what to do again and I'll finish the job those white boys couldn't do."

Paw Paw mumbled something.

"Fuck did you say, old man?"

Paw Paw slowly lifted his head and rested it on the oven door. Breathed through his gritted teeth.

"When I said, 'Don't kill him'... I wasn't talking to you."

Chapter 7,

Frederick

The security gig was the old days.

I'm now retired. No more of that bullshit daily grind for me. Got lucky and won the lottery. Got really lucky actually; that dumb nigger bitch I married up and left me and got herself a divorce. Before I won! Good riddance, cunt. She took the kid, too. Retard ex-wife come try and get me for my money after she saw me on the TV news for child support. Ha! Wasn't even sure it was mine. Who knows with that fat whore. So I got myself the best Jew lawyer in town. Looked in the phone book for the first Jew names I could find. Shut her down faster than a nun's legs. Guess what? Child support is based off of *earned* income. Lottery winnings ain't earned income. And I don't have a job. So she's getting jack squat. Fuck that bitch.

So now I frequent this strip club. The girls there are nice and young. And beautiful! Love me to death. Some of the slutty ones will give me hand jobs in the back. Only charge me two thousand. Seems like a fair price. Who cares? I got the bread to back me up. They won't kiss me, though. Probably cause of my missing teeth. I'll get that fixed next. Maybe marry one of the strippers. Live happily ever after, like in a fairytale.

Whatever. This was a fresh start as far as I was concerned. Didn't have to deal with any of them blacks no more. Didn't have to deal with them trashy whites in the trailer park either.

I moved away. Fuck em. Fuck em all. Moved to this nice, beautiful subdivision in the suburbs. A place where white, upstanding Americans like myself can live free from the scourge and suffering of lesser apes. I park my pickup truck right up on the front lawn and everything. Still with the Confederate flags. People know who the new boss on the block is.

Sometimes I have strippers and their friends over. Big ass parties. End up spending a boatload of money, but it don't matter. I won 1.2 million after taxes. After the house and all the toys I still have over two hundred thousand left over. That's two with a bunch of zeros behind it. Should be enough for the rest of my life. I even still get food stamps! Like I said, all this stuff is based on *earned* income. Lottery winnings ain't considered earned income.

Basically, I'm just a winner all the way around. Everyone knows it.

So there she was again. Every day at 3:17 PM. Walked right by the house on her way home from school. She was young, just a schoolgirl. But I knew when she filled out she'd be as ripe as a pumpkin. Sweet Lord; long curls, long legs, and that tight Catholic schoolgirl's outfit. Lord have mercy. I knew it was wrong, but looking never hurt nobody, right?

I open up the garage and set up a lawn chair in the driveway every day at three in preparation. Yell *HELLO!* as loud as I can when she walks by. Maybe I should invite her to one of my parties? Would she be able to sneak away? Would she be cool and not tell her parents? Maybe I could be her second daddy. Like an uncle. Treat her right like the princess she is. Kids can't talk to their parents about the important stuff these days. I could protect her. Be her guardian angel. And when the time is right, give her the love she deserves. I'm smart as Einstein so I should be able to figure out something.

Probably smarter.

So it was a hot day and I was out in the lawn chair as usual at three. Cracked open an ice-cold beer and waited for my daily show. She walked up on time as usual.

Hey, there! You! Schoolgirl!

She looked over. Gave her usual half-wave/head nod and kept walking.

Hey! Come over here, get a soda! Got plenty of 'em. It's hot and all out here.

"I need...to get home. Mom is expecting me. Thanks, though, sir."

Sir? You don't need to call me sir! I'm Frederick. I'm rich from the lottery. You probably saw me on the TV since I'm famous now. Come on over. Just take a minute. I'm new to the neighborhood. Just trying to be neighborly and friendly. You know, get to know some of the people on the block. You live what, four or five houses up? What's your name, sweetheart?

She stopped. YES! Got her now.

"Gracie."

I walked over and shook her hand. Soft. The hairs on my neck stood up. I'd been waiting for this moment for so long. And now it was here. I had to make sure to say the exact right words. Been practicing in the mirror for weeks now.

Gracie! What a beautiful name. Beautiful name for a beautiful girl.

"Uh, thanks. Why don't you park your truck in the driveway? Why do you park it on the lawn?"

So the neighborhood knows there's a new boss on the block, ha ha. You like it? I could take you for a ride around the block if you want. I'll even show you how to shift. Do you know about the shifting? It's something real men know how to do. That's why I know how to do it, you know. Because I'm a real man. I'm sure you noticed. I'm a real good driver, too. Only been in eight or nine accidents my whole life.

"No thanks. I, uh, don't have time to go for a ride right now. I got to get going home."

Well at least get your soda, over here in the garage!

She trailed behind me. Yes! We walked into the garage and I opened the fridge. She picked out a Mountain Dew.

Good choice, Gracie. You like Mountain Dew, huh? I can go to the store and get more. Maybe get a machine, too, just for you. That way you can quench your thirst every day after a long day at school. You stop by anytime you want and I'll have it, I promise. Even on the weekends. Do you like parties? I got lots of friends. And you could bring your friends. We could have a Mountain Dew party if you'd like. I'll tell you what, I'll just get some more tonight, that's for sure, okay?

"Look, um, thanks for the soda. I'm going to go now. I have to get home."

Just wait a second!

I had my laptop on the bench. I opened it up and went to my favorite website.

Look, Gracie, I'm gonna shoot straight with you. I've been think-ing about this for a long time. Been wanting to talk to you about this for a while now, see. See, I'm full of wisdom here on account of my age and the experiences I've had. And I've had lots. Especially recently after the lottery. So boys are going to come around to you real soon. They'll want to take you out on dates and such, you know, like movies or a nice dinner. At the end of the date, because you're so pretty, they'll want something from you, if you know what I mean.

"Um, no. I don't know what you mean."

I turned the laptop in her direction. Her eyes widened. I didn't want her to freak out so I slowed my talking speed. I really need her to *hear* what I was saying. Have her understand that I'm the only one willing to give her the real talk, one on one. I was her friend. I'm sure she understood that. I mean, how many people have offered to buy her a Mountain Dew machine?

Like sex stuff. It can be a big deal for someone young like you, so I'm here to help. Guide you. You can put in the search bar up here what you want to watch and the computer pulls it up. You know what a search bar is, sweetheart? I can show you if you want. I'm really smart with the computers. Smart with a lot of things, so if you have questions, feel free to fire away. I know this kind of stuff is hard to talk to your parents about, so Uncle Freddy is here to help, if you catch my drift. Anything sex stuff. And I mean anything. Hand jobs, blow jobs, like butt stuff, even sex with other races of people, believe it or not; anything you want. So when you're ready, I'll be here. I'm your friend, see.

She dropped the soda and ran off. The young ones are always shy at first. She'll come around. The next day I sat out as usual and

59

Gracie didn't show. Maybe she was sick or something. I'll have to get some Tylenol for her. Maybe some soup. Chicken noodle, maybe.

Chapter 8,

Randy

So I had a friend named Reeves. Thirty-five when he died. I didn't get mad when it happened. Just sad. I accepted it. I never expected him to live a long life, but I broke when I found out. I was all he had.

When he passed we had been friends for at least twenty years. We met for the first time at a church youth group. I was never religious, and neither were my parents. I was just there to try and hook up with this chick. I'd do anything to be around her. Even go to church. She was smokin' hot. Her name was Gracie. We never went out. Shit, I never even had a chance.

At the time Reeve's dad was in the hospital. Stage four cancer. He was in the hospital for about three months. Surprised he even made it that long. The church held special prayer services for him. They prayed for the cancer demons to leave his body. Raised their hands. Spoke in tongues. Anointment with oil. People became slain in the spirit and flopped around on the floor. The pastor would put his hand on the heads of the members of the congregation and they would drop like dead weight, some chanting, some screaming. Looked like something out of a horror film.

A bad horror film.

People stood up and prophesied his complete healing. Knowing without a doubt that one day he would walk back into the church cancer free. The audience cheered. Clapped. Cried. Hugged each other. Flopped around on the floor again.

I went to the last special healing service for Reeves' dad. The old man died a week later.

A few weeks after the funeral I invited him out for burgers after youth service. We went out and had a great time. He even laughed a bit. And that was the start of our friendship.

I soon found out that I was his only friend. He was very socially awkward, but for some reason, he latched on to me. I understood him, and he understood me. He never really got along with anyone else.

He never had a girlfriend. Thought he might be half a fag. I asked him about it. He didn't get mad. Assured me he wasn't. Said he was in a weird place with his family life, and church took up a lot of his time.

Whatever. No big deal.

As he grew older he had a more stressed relationship with his mom. He said they didn't agree on anything. He wanted to move, but always had financial problems. As the years went on nothing ever changed for him. Even after I was out of college he still lived with his mom, had the same low paying fast-food job, and went to the same church. I tried to help him out by giving him ideas for different jobs he could get, but every time I talked to him he just became more frustrated. He felt hopeless.

They went to church almost every day. Sunday morning they attended Sunday school and the regular service. Sunday night was always an evangelist session. Monday his mother and he went out to the neighborhood going door to door passing out gospel tracts or fliers to the next church event. Tuesday night was senior service (Reeves assisted with the wheelchairs). Wednesday night was a bible study service. At the Thursday night youth group they would assist the youth pastor with set up and help out with the worship portion. At the end of the service they'd help out with the clean up. Friday night he would go to the singles service. New people would show up and sometimes couples formed, but there was always a core group of misfits that never dated anyone, even though they'd go to the services for years on end. Saturdays consisted of some church event that Reeves and his mother would attend. And then Sunday it would start all over again.

We would have these long discussions about faith. He would question my faith, or lack thereof. How could I eat every meal without praying? How could I go a day without reading the bible? How could I not be scared of the rapture or Armageddon? He wondered what it would be like to not go to church for a week. Or to skip a service.

I'd explain that I've never felt the need for a savior. My sins were my own. I had to live with them. If you say some magic words nothing changes. The past is gone. You learn by making mistakes and doing your best not to repeat them. Live your life and try not to hurt others. Plus, I didn't want to spend all my free time going to all of those services and events.

Jesus said some of you will not taste death before my return. And yet here we still are. Waiting for his triumphant return. And waiting for the dead in Christ to rise again. Waiting. Every year there's some church (including his) that knew when Jesus was coming back in the twinkling of an eye. People sell all their property and possessions because they know the truth. In the end, no one shows up. They're still here just like the rest of us.

I'd explain that I wasn't indoctrinated as a child to worry about every action I took and every thought I had. Thought crime isn't a pretty picture. I wasn't taught to fear the flames of hell.

Because it's not real.

Years ago we'd be in youth service and everyone would cheer when the pastor talked about the heathens burning, and cheering that we would have reign over a new heaven and a new earth. Everyone else would burn for eternity because the most benevolent and loving creator must punish those who do not abide. And there were worms at some point.

I also explained that I love sleeping in on Sundays.

And that's why he was drawn to me originally. Because I was different from anyone he'd ever met.

He always said I acted like I was free.

I told him it wasn't an act.

Eventually we grew apart. After college, I got married. His mom wouldn't let him go to the wedding; it wasn't in a church. We moved about fifty miles up north. Not too far, but with his busy church schedule he couldn't ever come out to the house. I stopped in and checked on him when I went back into town, which was about twice a year. I'd have to drop by the burger stand or at the church since he was rarely home. We still talked on the phone every now and again, but he was distant. Tired.

I called him on his 35th birthday. He was unusually happy. So excited to hear from me. He had made a major life-changing decision.

He was finally leaving the church and moving out on his own. He wanted to meet up and talk about it.

I told him we need to celebrate. On me. Go on a trip. I had so many unused flight points I could get us anywhere in the U.S., hotel and car rental included. He responded with an emphatic yes. He needed to get away more than anyone. He'd never been on a plane before, or even left the state.

Time to branch out.

Get crazy. Cray Cray as fuck.

YOLO, as the kids say these days.

I suggested San Francisco. I was there a few years ago for a bachelor party. I only stayed one night and was shit-housed the entire time. I always wanted to go back and explore. I was sure Reeves would dig it.

So I received permission from the wife and booked the trip. Took off a week from work and off we went. We left on a Sunday and we were coming back the following Sunday. I promised him no church. At all. If we drove by a church he'd have to close his eyes.

We had the best time.

He talked to people. He talked to women. Drank beer. Tried to smoke a cigarette. Didn't work out in his favor. He choked. I laughed.

Every day we would hit up another famous attraction.

Fisherman's wharf.

Chinatown.

The Exploratorium.

The Aquarium of the Bay.

Alcatraz.

Golden Gate Bridge.

The Bridge was his favorite.

At dinner that evening he was unusually quiet. He seemed on edge about something. As we walked back to the hotel I asked what was bothering him.

He talked about the church, and how his whole life revolved around it. His whole existence was to make sure he was right with God. And only through God you could have peace. And there he was, a world away from it all, and at 35 years old, he felt peace for the first time in his life.

He went on to talk about the 'problem' between him and his mom. He would pray and pray and pray. Twenty fucking years had gone by and God never answered his cries for help. This frustrated him to no end. He realized the only way to solve the problem was to rely on himself.

I asked what problem he and his mom had for the past two decades. Asked why he had never talked to me about it before. We talked about damn near everything else throughout the years. I assumed it had to do with how many hours he was at the church each week, or possibly communication issues.

I was wrong.

I listened in horror as he calmly told me that his mom every so often would sneak into his room and jack him off while he slept. He'd wake up in the middle of it and his mom would be at his bedside stroking his cock and whispering his dad's name. She would smile and have one hand raised praising the Holy Father. If he was lucky he'd wake up before he ejaculated and kick her out. He begged her to stop. Pleaded. She said if he ever left she'd tell the church he was a sexual deviant. A pervert. Everyone he ever knew would know he was living in sin.

The cross was too heavy to bear. Church was all he knew.

Until now. Fuck all that.

I told him he was moving in with me immediately. I'd help him get back on his feet. The company I worked for was hiring warehouse staff and I knew I could get him a job. I knew a few doctors that could lead me in the right direction to get him some mental help.

He was so happy.

He wasn't going to take shit from her anymore. He didn't care what she told the church. At the end of our dinner he said he was moving on to the next step. I was heartbroken, but happy for him.

The next morning I woke up alone in the hotel. I slept in late. It was a little after ten.

Figured he went down to breakfast.

Maybe out for a walk.

I noticed a note on the hotel stationary on my nightstand, next to the Gideon Bible.

Yo!!!
What a great week. Thank you forever for
taking me out to this amazing place.
The food! The women! The freedom! I'm
sorry, but I'm leaving now. It's about
6am, and the sun is coming up. I'm going
back up to the bridge. By now I'm
long gone. Thanks for being my only friend.
For listening. For actually answering

my prayers. As your favorite book says, I got
you to look after me, and you got me
to look after you. Well, you don't have to
look after me anymore. I'm not leaving
because I want to die, I just need to ask God why.
-R

I sat on the bed and broke down crying.

Now I was the one asking God, why? I knew I was too late; that he was gone. I knew in my heart he had gone through with it. I could see it in my mind, clear as day. Him looking back and forth, waiting until no one was around to try and stop him. Hopping the rail, looking to the sky one last time. Breathing in the early morning bay air and smiling. Letting go with one hand and reaching out with the other, as if he could touch something, feel something, be alive one last time before letting go.

Chapter 9,

Gracie

I was lost and didn't want to talk to him, but couldn't talk to mom. I was confused. Scared. I went to the one person I knew that wasn't scared of anything. I opened the basement door and knocked on the wall.

Dad? Can I come down?

"Yeah! Come on down, kid. What's going on? I'm about to head out. About to meet some of the guys. You know, business stuff. Well, first Ma's gonna yell at me, then I'm gonna go. You know the routine, heh heh."

He was in a good mood, so that was a plus. I was about to ruin that, but I didn't have anywhere to turn. If I told mom, the police might get involved. Or she'd tell Dad, and Dad would get mad at me. Dad was going to get mad at me no matter what, so I guess it didn't matter.

"Sit down, what's on your mind?"

He was finishing a beer. He dropped it in the trash can and the glass clanked and rattled with the other empty beer bottles that were already in there. I sat. He sat down next to me. I was scared. I knew he was going to be mad. But I hoped he could help me. At least Dad could talk to him. I hated walking home from the bus stop. That man was always there, in his driveway, like he was waiting for me. There was no real way to avoid his house; we were in a cul-de-sac on the edge of a subdivision surrounded by the woods. To go around I would have to hop backyards or traverse the thicket in the woods and still hop my own fence. So I opted to just be polite and neighborly and deal with the weird guy a few doors down. But enough was enough.

Dad, I just want to say...could you not get mad. Please don't get mad at me, okay?

"Mad about what? What did you fucking do?"

Please, Dad. Listen. So there's this guy.

"At school? You got a problem with a boy at school? What's his name. I'll talk to him. No big deal." He smiled.

No. Not at school. There's a guy down the block. The lotto winner?

"That fucking loser? That house is gonna be trash in two years. Faggot always leaves his big truck out, thinking he's a somebody. I swear to god, he peels out one more time I'm going over there." He leaned forward and pointed at me. "You know I fucking mean it. He bothering you or something? I fucking swear to god, Gracie, don't tell me he's bothering you. I *fucking* swear to god."

He was getting mad. When he was mad, he made this weird frown while gritting his teeth and shook his head 'no'.

I nodded yes.

"That son of a bitch; I fucking swear to god!"

70

So every day I walk home from the bus stop and walk up the street. He's in his garage in a lawn chair waving at me. I just ignore him and walk by. And yesterday he invited me in the garage for a soda.

"What did you do, Gracie? The fuck is going on here?" He stood up.

Look, um, he showed me a weird, um, porn site on his laptop and said...like... some weird sex things to me? And then I ran off. That's it. That's all. He didn't like touch me or anything, I swear. I just want him to leave me alone.

Dad stood up. He slapped me in the back of the head so hard. I fell to the ground. He pulled me back to my feet by my ponytail. "YOU DUMB FUCKING IDIOT! THE FUCK IS WRONG WITH YOU? YOU ARE SO FUCKING STUPID, I SWEAR TO GOD!"

He pushed me to the ground. I lay on the ground, crying.

He picked up the phone and called someone. "Yeah, I'm not gonna make it tonight til later on. Yeah? Well, I don't give a fuck. I got some stuff to take care of. Fuck off and handle it til I get there, you fucking dope. Deal with it...I SAID DEAL WITH IT!"

Dad doesn't like to be questioned.

At all.

Chapter 10,

Robbie

So at a garage sale awhile back Paw Paw and I got a cast iron skillet for two bucks. I thought he was crazy spendin' that much bread on an old piece of junk, especially since it was all rusted out. Complete garbage. Paw Paw assured me it was a great deal. A few days later he showed up at the apartment with the pan. Looked completely different. Didn't even believe it was the same one.

"You know Jimmy the Tooth? He work down there over at that machine shop on Broadway. He owed me a favor; had him sandblast the rust off this pan. Now we're not going to cook with it just yet. We don't want it to rust out again. We got to season the pan first."

Season, like salt and pepper?

"No no no. When you have a pan like this you need to oil it up with fancy-ass oil and then bake it into the pores of the metal. Then you have a pan you can use for the rest of your life. It takes a little more love to keep one of these alive, but I promise you you'll be able to tell the difference. Especially with meats. This one is seventy plus years old, can you believe that? It's my gift to you, kid. Got this grape seed oil-"

What's grape seed oil?

"It's oil from grape seeds, nigga. What the fuck you think it is?"

Chapter 11,

Frederick

That night there was a knock at the door. I was kind of drunk, waiting for my Asian delight. The escort service was sending me an Asian this time! Planned on sticking it in her ass unexpectedly to hear her scream and cry. That was always my favorite. Having them yell and try and hit you so you pull out. Never works. I'm the boss. I do what I want. If they yell too loud I just punch them in the back of the head continually until they shut up. I get mine whether they like it or not. I'm the one paying, right? I deserve to have a good time and get my money's worth. Whores. Who cares about them. And who are they going to complain to? She was supposed to be here around 11:30. It was only 10:30 now. An hour early! I wasn't even close to being ready yet.

Wait a minute! I'll be there in a minute!

I stumbled to my room. Grabbed a Viagra and washed it down with a beer on the dresser that had been there for who knows how long. Lit a cigarette. Walked back to the front and opened the door.

Who the fuck are you?

"Well, I heard there was a new boss on the block and wanted to say hello."

Okay, uh, hello, yes, that's me. Now get the fuck out of here. I'm busy. Expecting some company soon.

"How soon?"

Not that it's any of your goddamned business, but in about an hour.

"Oh, good. We have plenty of time." He smiled at me.

Time for what? Who the fuck are you? Get the fuck off my porch before I whoop your ass, you piece of shit. You don't know who the fuck you're dealing with.

"I'm Gracie's dad."

Oh shit. Gracie's dad.

Listen, pal; it ain't what you think! Stop pushing me! Let go! I can explain! It ain't what you thi-

Chapter 12,

Reeves

Mother never worked. Stayed home all the time, other than church. At our apartment she had two duties. Her first duty was to pray over our home, an exercise she took to heart. She probably prayed at least six hours total throughout the average day.

She'd start at about five a.m. She would begin by crying. Loud. Speaking in tongues. She'd lay on the living room floor rolling around screaming, pleading for God to let no harm fall upon us. By the time we awoke she sat waiting for us. Father and I would get on our knees and she would anoint our heads with oil. Basically she would dip her finger in olive oil and make crosses on our foreheads.

We bought the olive oil from the store in bulk. On Sunday afternoons we would go to the pastor's house so he could bless the case of oil with an anointing from the Holy Spirit. Every day the windows and front door would be open and Mother would cast out the demons that would gather in the house overnight.

Demons in the living room.

Demons in the kitchen.

Demons in the bedroom.

Waiting. Waiting for us to falter. Waiting for us to not be ready. The very second we doubted or sinned these demons would take complete control of our bodies and make sure during the end times we would accept the mark of the beast.

Father lost his job last year so for a bit we had to use vegetable oil. I hope the demons didn't notice.

Her second duty was to educate me.

Home school.

We would do lessons for about an hour a day. And then about eight hours of the important stuff.

The Bible. Reading. Studying. Praying. Workbooks. More praying. If I was lucky sometimes we would listen to church sermons on the AM radio. I loved the AM radio. Mother let me listen to it at least three times a year. What a thrill.

Father could never keep a job for that long. He always had the same excuses.

The boss didn't like him.

Too many hours.

The other employees were out to get him.

They didn't allow sufficient breaks for prayer.

And it was always 'they'. I never actually knew who the 'they' was, but 'they' sure had it in for Father.

Apparently companies do not appreciate employees exorcising customers during business hours.

Father would get on unemployment and right about the time the unemployment was up he'd happen to magically find a new job.

By the grace of God.

Manna from Heaven.

Eventually he found a job as a custodian at a smaller elementary school. He loved it. No one was around to harass him because he worked the night shift alone.

* * *

So one Saturday we had three things to do.

First, Bible study and prayer for at least five hours.

Second, we were going to look at a small house to see if we'd like to buy it. Now that Father appeared to have a stable employment Mother suggested we move out of the apartment. She hated living in a 'grid of demons', as she called it.

Third, we were going to a sermon in the next town over. The church had a special guest Father knew from back in the day and he was so excited to finally reconnect with an old friend.

So once prayer was out of the way, we drove to the house to check it out.

We had heard about it from a couple at church. The couple's friends were selling the house below market value. Robert and Susan. They had just retired and bought a house boat. Selling their house was the last obstacle they faced before leaving for the gulf.

The house was very small. One level. Maybe nine hundred square feet. There were three small bedrooms and one bathroom. They were selling the house for $36,000. Also, they were going to take care of all the closing costs. Even though it was a below market price, no offers had been made.

We met them in the afternoon for a tour of the home. As we walked through the rooms, Mother asked why the house was still furnished. All of the couches, tables, and beds were still in all the rooms. Susan explained that everything, furniture and appliances, came with the house. They were moving on the boat and had no use for any of it, and didn't want the hassle of paying someone to take it or selling individual pieces. Susan told Mother if they bought the house they could keep the items, sell them, or give them away.

Mother promptly stated that she didn't like the couch. Susan explained again. If they didn't want anything in the house they could do as they wished.

Keep.

Sell.

Give away.

Throw away.

They didn't care.

And then Mother saw it. She gasped. Asked Father to hold her. Prayed for the Blood of Jesus. I saw it too. I started to sweat. I had no clue how Mother would react. She began to shake and cry. Father put his arms around her and told her everything was going to be okay.

Mother asked Susan why she had a devil box.

"I'm sorry, what? What is a devil box? What?" Susan looked at her husband confused. Robert was beginning to get annoyed.

Mother slowly picked up her shaking arm and pointed to the Nintendo on top of the television.

Susan explained that when her grandchildren were younger they would come over and sometimes play games.

Mother did not approve. She made sure Susan knew what was up.

"Video games? Are you joking? Video games are a distraction from the work of our Lord and Savior Jesus Christ. See, Satan travels from continent to continent luring the youth of our world in various ways to eternal damnation. Video games *specifically* were designed to pave the way to hell for the souls of the lost. Straight. To. Hell. With worms and eternal gnashing of teeth. When Christ rides in on a flying white horse of JUSTICE he will raise the dead in Christ and at the same time vanquish all who oppose him, and all that have pledged allegiance to their lord and savior Beelzebub, Lucifer, Diablos, or whatever you call the Prince of Darkness. You want to play games? I suggest you don't play games with your eternal soul. That's why it is eternal. Because you will have to live forever knowing that you personally have helped the true God and King of Kings himself erase names from the Lamb's Book of Life due to your lacking of faith and weak composure. A time when Children are supposed to be innocent and free you have strengthened the future chains of bondage upon the youth of this great nation. You have knowingly tampered and interfered with their path on the straight and narrow and given a helping detour to a place with fiery coals."

Mother raised her voice.

"Have you not seen the news? AIDS? Malaria? Smallpox? You think these diseases are accidents? There are earthquakes around the world, Susan. Earthquakes. And tsunamis. And you sit here smug in your castle high above the rest of us thinking that no one will come to your door, knock, and warn you about impending judgment? Well guess what? A PROPHETESS IS HERE. Heed my word, child, and the Lord shall give you a revelation of true soul healing and belonging. An inner peace from the conflict and struggle in your heart. Now. And if you didn't know you were a sinner five minutes ago you do now. You are no longer innocent or ignorant of the truth. I am here to guide you. Put you on the true path of righteousness, for His name's sake. Amen. Amen. Amen. It's not just throwing away the devil box. Now we need to pray the evil away and God can bring his holy blood and wash this tainted home from all you have brought upon us. We are all guilty now. We all need a savior. Susan and Robert, please grab my hands and let us pray to the almighty."

Mother closed her eyes and held out her hands. There was an eerie silence in the air. After a few moments Robert and Susan asked us to leave. Father shook his head. "Heathens." He looked back as we walked toward the door.

"When you change your mind give us a call. And that Nintendo better not be here, understand? We prayed about this house. It's called ask and you shall receive. Maybe you idiots should read the good book."

They never called.

We continued our day by going to the church. They were having a revival that night. The building was small and rundown. It looked as if a stiff breeze could blow it over. The paint was all chipped and potholes littered the parking lot. Inside was the ugliest stained orange carpet I had ever seen. The place smelled of dirty laundry.

About thirty beat up and dented metal chairs faced a makeshift stage. We were the first so we naturally had to sit in the front row.

We were waiting for the guest speaker that night, Willie Vickers. You may remember him from the papers. Back in '94 he was caught having an affair with a male foreign exchange student. After harsh criticism, he faced the public. He explained that demons of darkness tempted him with the flesh. It's okay now, because Jesus had cured him from being a 'gay'. No more gay, in Jesus' name.

He started gay conversion therapy seminars and toured the country. He would transform gay Christian men into normal Christian men by exorcising the gay demons out of them. The seminars cost three thousand a person. Sure, that may be a lot of money, but what costs more? Three thousand? Or your eternal soul?

Eventually Willie stopped his roadshow circus and started a church up in Colorado Springs. One of those fancy mega churches built like a stadium. He did all of the gay conversion on site. He made more money by having the gays come to him. He still traveled once a year doing revivals to promote the church and its services, which is why he was in town.

To save the lost. To eradicate the gay from the heart of America.

Father lived in Colorado Springs years before I was born. He attended Willie's church. All my life I heard the stories of the revivals, healing, exorcisms, speaking in tongues, and all that jazz. The gay conversion even had their own slogan.

'Feel Jesus. Let him come inside you'.

About twenty people came out for this revival. The pastor of the church came out and welcomed everyone for visiting, and then introduced Willie's band, Straight Edge.

The band started playing. Willie jumped on the stage and began singing, dancing, raising his hands, and clapping to get the crowd all excited for the power of Jesus.

Something was a bit off with the drummer. He was an overweight hairy balding white guy in his mid-forties. While the rest of the band was wearing a shirt and tie, he was in cutoff jean shorts and a dirty tank top. He was sweating profusely. His timing was off as well. The band would have to slow down or speed up to match the beat.

And then he would scream. Twitch uncontrollably. Grit his teeth. He yelled something and dropped his drum sticks. I couldn't hear what he yelled because of the volume of the music.

Later I found out that his condition was called Tourette Syndrome. He would scream and shake. The band paid no attention. Willie paid no attention. He'd freak out and when he composed himself he'd jump back into the music.

At the end of the worship service, Willie led the congregation in prayer. While he prayed, the drummer had a fit. "FUCK! Fuckityshitfuck. UGHHHH. Niggerfuckity!" He hit a cymbal with the drumstick. The crowd gasped. Pastor Willie kept praying as if nothing happened. I looked around. Everyone was shocked. After a few seconds people looked back down in prayer. When Pastor Willie was done praying he began his sermon, but everyone had eyes on the drummer.

He had another fit. "Fuckityfuckfuck! Hehhhhughhh. Ugh! Turkeyniggerturkeynigger. UGH!" He twitched so hard he threw a drumstick into the crowd. It hit Mother in the neck. She was not amused. She coughed as she collapsed and Father helped her up. She immediately walked out. Father followed, leaving me in the front row, about ten feet from the drummer. I started to pray. I might be next. The drummer composed himself. He walked over, quietly apologized to me and retrieved the drum stick. Father came back alone after a few minutes. Mother would wait in the car for the remainder of the service.

Pastor Willie preached the rest of his sermon. The drummer had multiple outbursts. Every time, the crowd would jump back.

After the service we went to the car to get Mother. She was irate. Father wanted Mother to meet Willie. She eventually agreed and we met Willie by the front entrance. Willie shook her hand. "Ma'am, I'm so sorry about Jackson. We've been praying a long time for the demons that make him shake to leave his body, but his faith level just hasn't been where it needs to be. Once he gets there? Poof! He'll be transformed in the twinkling of an eye." He smiled. Mother was not impressed. Willie turned to Father. "But hey it's good to see you, little buddy! Been a long time. Glad to see you've stuck to the program. You're a testament of the good work we're doing for the Lord."

Mother looked confused. "What program? What are you talking about?" Mother looked at Father. "What is he talking about, Lance?" Father was red in the face. He looked down.

Willie patted Father on the back. He had the biggest smile on his face. "Well Lance here was our first success in our gay conversion therapy!"

Chapter 13,

Gracie

Where are we going, dad?

"The Lawn and Garden shop. Get some soil. Fill in that hole out back."

I knew people usually had lots of soil delivered, so I asked, Why don't we get the soil delivered, like in a big dump truck?

"You think I have time to set shit up like that? We'll do it ourselves. And quit asking so many fucking questions. I know what I'm doing. A man makes his own way. If he can take care of it himself, he does so. Not rely on some asshole to show up late and jack you around for a few bucks. And then that asshole you don't know now knows where you live. *Get it delivered*. You got to be fucking kidding me."

Won't the car be a mess?

"It's all in bags. Jesus. You know, in those big plastic fifty-pound bags? No mess. We'll put as many as we can in the trunk and in the back seat. Should be fine. No big deal. Maybe a few on your lap on the way back if you don't shut your trap."

I knew one car load of soil wouldn't be enough. We had a new roof put on the house a few weeks ago. Big job. Took a few days. We opened the big gate on the back side to let one of the roofing company's trucks in so the ladders could be set up. The grass on the front driver's side started to sink. The driver backed out in time to not be swallowed up. Underneath was an old hollow septic tank, no longer in use, that had caved in once the truck tried to drive over it. Dad covered it up with a few sheets of plywood that were in the garage that had been left by the previous owners. For weeks and weeks nothing was done about the hole. Mom added that to the list of things they argued about every day. Finally Dad was going to do something about it.

We left the lawn and garden shop with twenty two bags. One of the bags tore open in the back seat. Dad was not happy. "God dammit."

I opened the big gate to the back and he drove close to the boarded up hole. I went and started to remove the plywood. Something stank. Bad. Like a dead animal was somewhere in the backyard.

"Hey! Don't touch the plywood! I'll do that later! Help me get the bags out. We'll make a pile. Looks like it's not gonna be enough. I'll have to make a few more trips."

I can start filling the hole while you get more soil. Or we can dump these bags in now and go back. Do you smell something, Dad?

"No, uh, don't smell nothing. Um, Look, kid, I want to do this by myself. I don't want you to.... um, you know, fall in the hole and get hurt or something, okay? Let's just stack all the bags in a pile."

We stacked all the bags in a pile. Like a really shitty small pyramid. Was Dad hiding something? He usually didn't talk to me like this.

"And I'm sorry about the other day. I snapped. I just, ya know, love you and I want you to be safe. Between work and your Ma, always busting my fucking chops, you're the only light I have in my life."

Now I knew something was off. He'd never told me he loved me. Ever. I maintained a straight face but inside I was broken. Or lifted up? I can't explain the feeling. I wanted to cry. Wanted to scream. Wanted to hug him. Hold him. Tell him I loved him, too. Was this happiness? After all this time was there finally a connection being made?

I did none of those things.

I understand, Dad.

I folded my arms and walked away, back into the house and into the little sunroom where Mother had all her plants. My favorite place to read. My book sat on the little deck chair and I picked it up, but just looked out the window. Dad lifted the plywood. Covered his face and fanned his arm trying to repel an odor. I knew something smelled bad. Probably a dead squirrel or raccoon in there. He took a pocket knife out of his jacket and started cutting the bags. The pocket knife I got for him for Christmas a few years ago. Never thought he would have had it on him. He poured the dirt in, bag by bag.

The soil smell never left the Lincoln, no matter how much we vacuumed or wiped down. I was right; we needed way more bags to fill the holes. Over the next few days he went by himself to the Lawn and Garden shop to get more bags.

Dad had the hole filled after about a week. A week after the hole was filled word got out in the neighborhood that the lotto winner had disappeared. No trace of him. A month later the city towed his truck from the front lawn.

After the hole was filled Dad made a comment to me that everything was going to be okay.

No one was going to bother me anymore.

Chapter 14,

Reeves

In the old days there was this mega church close to where I grew up. The place could hold ten thousand people or so for each service. Each summer they held a camp for the 'Soldiers of Christ'.

Milton ran the camp. He was an old-timer that did two tours in 'Nam. A genuine badass (pardon my language) fluent in the language of firearms and hand to hand combat.

Camp was located on his property about forty miles west of town towards the mountains. People from all over the country would spend one to two weeks of the summer learning outdoor survival, hand to hand combat, and guns.

Guns. Guns. Guns.

You'd do your time at camp and the rest of the year you would enroll in whatever self-defense classes that were available in your hometown.

During the summer my parents would send me to Milton's camp to be his assistant. I started the summer after first grade.

At first I was the caretaker of the guns. Every make. Every model. Every caliber. Cleaning. How to take apart and put back together. How to reload ammunition. After two summers I began training in hand to hand combat. This also included weapons: knives, swords, batons.

He also taught me how to box. That's where I excelled. I trained a minimum of five hours a day each summer boxing once I turned nine. Dieting, lifting, running, heavy hitting, sparring. Didn't even have Sundays off. On Sundays I'd just have to get up earlier and do a half practice before church and the other half after.

Services at the camp were exactly the same as at church.

We showed up and we were greeted.

Newcomers were welcome.

We gave an offering.

We did the communion and drank from the cup.

Ate the bread.

The music started. Slow at first. Some people sat. Others stood.

A faster song would start.

Everyone stood and clapped.

Raised their hands.

Jumped up and down.

Listened to a message.

And then everyone would leave.

My disarming skills are second to none. I can disarm anyone with damn near any weapon with precision and accuracy. By the time they blink I already have their gun, knife, baton, or hammer away from them. In some of our firearm disarming training we would use loaded guns.

Years of combat training led to the follower's final test in an area of the camp known as 'The City'. It was a secluded area with old trailers, pallets, and sheds set up like a residential street. The goal was to walk down the street and fight off all attackers. Ten other students would be hiding out as you walked through with various weapons and attack you, usually two at a time.

At the end of the block Milton had a giant gong. If you made it you'd strike the gong and Milton and the other followers that had passed the test in the past would come out and hug you. And then they would sit at this picnic table and eat a 'Jesus Melon'. It was just a watermelon from the garden. He'd cut it up for everyone and pass out the pieces and they'd laugh and talk about the old days. And pray. Lots of praying.

I remember being so confused when I passed my walk. I sat on a bucket by the picnic table all bloodied and beaten, missing two teeth, eating a piece of watermelon, while Milton cried and danced before the Lord with fresh melon juice running down his chin.

It did taste good, though. After a beating your senses are height-ened. You can *feel* the air. Each muscle. Each heartbeat. Taste the salt of the blood and the sweetness of the melon. Nothing like it.

Most followers thought they could make it after training for five summers; most were wrong.

Some had to take two or three tries, and you could only make a go of it once a summer. I failed my first try, actually. I had been training hard for six years, so I thought by the time I was thirteen I could make it. I had grown that last winter and was over five feet tall, and probably 115 pounds of pure muscle.

The seventh follower had clocked me in my right ear with a fairly long two by four. Student two had already cut my left hand and broke at least two ribs. Follower five I actually knew. His name was Jim. He was a deacon at the church. Taught tenth grade British Literature. Always had a smile on his face. And he could hit. Hard.

I limped past a shed and he popped out in front of me and hit me with a hard right cross. Right in the jaw. Almost blacked out. We fought for about thirty seconds. Doesn't sound like a long time, but for me, it was an eternity. I was Milton's prodigy, so all the followers that day were trying extra hard to take me out. Jim wanted so much to be in Milton's' good graces. Be a part of his 'elite squad'. Taking me out would be his ticket to the top. Stopping someone from getting to the gong and melon was highly coveted.

He didn't beat me though. I got him with two clean hits to the face and one sloppy hit to the neck. Split the cut on my hand wider. Blood poured out faster.

He dropped and couldn't breathe. I put him in a headlock.

He squirmed.

Elbowed me in my broken ribs.

Tried to scratch my face.

Cried.

Not this year, Jim, I thought.

His body went limp and I set him down gently. Other than all the blood on his face (some his, some mine), he looked so peaceful as he slept in the leaves. I did feel bad. He was such a nice guy.

After student seven hit me with the two by four I fell hard. He hit me again in the back so hard the two by four broke in half. We wrestled for a bit, but he was more skilled than me. Eventually he hit me hard. My face fell into a pile of chopped wood. He kicked me in the gut so hard. I blamed myself. I'd made a fool of myself. And Milton.

I woke up in my tent. No clue how long I had been there. My arm was crudely stitched and a bandage was on my head. Everything hurt. The camp didn't believe in medicine. Only prayer.

Milton sat next to my cot. His hands were in his palms. He wept softly. He looked up at me in disgust. "You know what happens out there in the cities now? Biblical prophecy, that's what. You think it's all fun and games out there. How are you going to survive, huh?"

The tears streamed down his face. "Every day, roving bands of homosexuals prowl the streets looking for weak targets, weak targets like you, to capture and rape."

He poked me in the ribs. I groaned. Coughed up a little blood. He looked up and tried to compose himself. He took a deep breath. "Faggots looking for weak targets. A literal Sodom and Gomorrah. Gays, whores, witches, all out there casting demonic spells of dark magic to the masses. Christians murdered every day here in America. Worse than Hitler's little Holocaust. The Jews had it easy compared to what we are going through out there. Because ours is a battle for the soul. I'd gladly suffer in a little gas chamber because I know! I know for a fact! That when I die I will be reunited with my heavenly father! Because our war is for the spirit! Our battle is for the soul! You think this is a game? How can you make it out there? You can't even fight ten people! Ten!"

He hugged me. Which hurt worse than the shot to the ribs. "If you were in a real city you would have been kidnapped and raped. Look at me. They would have kidnapped you and put your organs on the black market. Do you know what the black market is? It's where black people buy illegal things. Is that what you want?"

I shook my head no.

Milton was a true bible thumper. In the worst way. Everyone he met he invited to church. Everyone. At the supermarket. The doctor's office. The bus. Even people at church that were already at church.

Now, there is nothing wrong with sharing your beliefs. It's just the way he went about it. If people were in a rush or politely declined he would get loud. Angry. Belligerent. Nasty. Talk down to them. Call them idiots. Fools. Yell at them about the end times and how they would suffer eternal hellfire.

All he ever talked about was the book of Revelations. The rapture. "I'll be taken into glory! Like a thief in the night!" It was his whole life. Any topic brought up he'd twist the conversation somehow back to the bible and end times prophecy.

Milton's brother Greg was at church once and showed Milton a picture of his niece. "She's beautiful," he responded. "Too bad she'll be taken during the rapture because she's innocent and you' be stuck here fighting for your life during the battle of Armageddon. Ever think about that, Greg? Why don't you stop showing off pictures and start showing people your true colors for Christ and pass out biblical tracts? Might get you in better with the big guy upstairs, if you know what I mean. Glad I could help. Idiot."

"I'll be taken into Glory! Like a thief in the night!"

He repeated these lines so many times. Members of the church would avoid him. Some even made fun of him behind his back.

He would also sneak up on people at church. The idea was that as a Christian, you need to be ready at all times for the end of the world. If you weren't ready, you'd go to hell. He'd sneak up at church and yell. People would jolt. Scream. Throw their bibles in the air.

His tricks became more elaborate. He'd hide in trash cans and closets, sometimes all night just to have the proper effect. He always compared his nonsense to how no one knows the day, nor the hour, when Jesus will return.

"I'll be taken into glory! Like a thief in the night!"

He even tried to talk the pastor into taking the congregation hostage. He wanted to bring in his AK-47 and a ski mask and round up everyone during the prayer portion of the Sunday morning service. Shoot the joint up with blank rounds. Because that's how it will be when you get left behind.

He wanted everyone to be soldiers of Christ.

Pastor said no. Thank God.

Milton's cousin David was the same way.

One person that actually liked David was my dad. David would come over sometimes after church for lunch. He and Dad would have lengthy discussions about the end times. Every political and weather story on the news was sure to be a fulfillment of prophecy. They'd get out their bibles, look up verses, and run out into the street to try and round up the neighbors to show what the almighty savior had shown them. They would always bring up the fact of how happy they would be in Heaven while everyone on Earth died a horrible death due to war, famine, or disease.

Outside of town there's an abandoned lumber mill. Beside it is a lush wooded area with the most beautiful creek running by the largest building. People go there all the time. There're trails on both sides of the creek, so you get your runners, hikers, and fishermen. In the abandoned buildings youngsters hang out. They'll throw parties sometimes, drink, smoke dope, all that good stuff.

So one day the parents go to a couples' luncheon at the church. David was single, and I needed a babysitter, so we unfortunately ended up together for the afternoon.

David made a few brown bag lunches and we drove up to the mill to go for a hike. At first things were fine. We walked and he talked about God's creation. We found a nice grassy spot under a tree and ate. The sandwiches he made were actually delicious. As we ate, he blabbed on and on about the tribes of Judah, signs of the times, and other bible stories and how they applied to his personal life. I hadn't said a word all day. He liked to hear himself talk, I guess.

After lunch things became awkward. He began preaching to the other hikers and fishermen, passing out tracts and harassing them. His favorite tract was disguised to look like a folded fifty dollar bill. He'd put one on the trail and we'd hide in the bushes or behind a tree and wait. Inside the tract was a message of hope for salvation. A jogger would come along and pick it up, smile, open it up, and yell, "Fuck!" Then he or she would throw it down and we'd wait again. Like I said, inside was a message of salvation. Zero souls were saved that day.

So eventually on the way back to the car we ended up at a spot where you can cross the creek by jumping from rock to rock. There were six or seven rocks to make it across. David crossed and I followed slowly; my balance wasn't the best and I wasn't a skilled swimmer. He yelled at me when he made it to the other side.

"Are you ready?!"

I wasn't sure what I was supposed to be ready for. I still had three rocks before I hit dry ground. I was concentrating on my next jump. The rock wasn't that flat, so I didn't want to slip. He pulled a Frisbee from his backpack. Threw it at me as hard as he could. I was maybe eight feet away, at best. As the Frisbee shattered my nose

I almost blacked out. I opened my eyes and realized I was floating downstream. I couldn't move. I watched the Frisbee float past. David jumped in and 'saved' me.

As I cried he tried to calm me. "See? It's okay buddy! Don't cry!" He smiled at me. "You should be thanking me. The Frisbee was unexpected, right? Just like the second coming of our Lord and Savior. No one knows the day or the hour! Like a thief in the night! Praise the Lord!"

He smiled as he drove me to the emergency room. He was so glad that he was able to teach me my most valuable lesson.

Of course Mom and Dad agreed with him. As David told my dad what happened my dad looked down and shook his head in disgust. If only I had been paying attention I could have been ready for anything coming my way. Three weeks after nasal surgery I could almost breathe correctly again. My black eyes were almost healed. Gracie at church also had bandages on her face the same time as me. I always wondered how she broke her nose. Hers was a lot worse than mine.

A few weeks later David came over to the house. He needed to talk to Dad. It's important, he said. David and Dad went into the den. Began to pray. Cry. Scream. They came out of the den about two hours later.

David announced to mom and I that he had received a revelation from God. The church needs to know.

So Sunday David got permission to speak to the congregation. He tells of how his grandmother passed away a few years back and left him a box of gold coins. Of course he gave his ten percent to the church, but was unsure of what to do with the rest. So it sat. Then he received a vision from Jesus. His mission was simple. Go to Israel and give the box of gold to the first Rabbi at the closest synagogue from his hotel. The purpose of this mission? He did not know. Jesus would reveal it. It was his journey. His penance. His pilgrimage.

So he bought a ticket to Jerusalem. And in typical David fashion, he tells everyone he encounters about Jesus and his dream. Including the cab driver on the way to the hotel.

Later that night the cab driver and his buddies broke into his hotel room and beat him within an inch of his life. They took the gold.

He must have not been ready.

He must have not been paying attention.

He was beaten and robbed.

By a thief in the night.

Chapter 15,

Robbie

I leaned down in front of Paw Paw. More blood seeping out from somewhere.

"Now I done told you. I told you I don't want you endin' up like me. I'm old, ain't much time left, 'specially now. I know I told you a mean dog gotta be put down, but you don't want to get a taste for it, like I got. You don't see what I see. How you gotta chance now. Keep your head down. I make no bones about it, it ain't easy. Stay down, now. Run outta here, boy. Leave me be. Don't feel bad about it. You go down this path there's no turnin' back."

Paw Paw knew what I was thinking.

"Kid, come on. Don't be like me."

Ray Ray sat on the couch and lit a cigarette. "Nigga, imma count to three, nigga, and you best have my money."

I picked up the cast iron pan. Squeezed the handle. All my troubles were now over. I could feel my blood flowing. Feel the heat in the air. For the first time, I had no fear. I was sick and tired of being sick and tired. Tired of going to school with dirty clothes. Tired of paying for food with food stamps, checking to see if the things we bought would be covered by the government's standards. Tired of little brother getting made fun of for being a half breed. Blacks don't like him cause he's light-skinned; white folk think he's a nigger. Tired of sitting at the bank on the first of the month, like clockwork, waiting with all those other worthless fools to cash that government bread.

"One."

Little brother walked out into the living room.

GO BACK TO BED, NIGGA!

He obediently walked back to our room. Good for him. He'll make it through foster care. Hopefully, because of his good behavior, he'll get adopted.

"Two."

Fuck you.

"What you say to me, nig-"

Paw Paw also taught me how to play baseball. How to catch, how to throw. How when I swing the bat I need to follow through so the ball goes further.

Swing *through* the ball, Paw Paw would say. Or I could swing through the head, with a cast iron pan.

I hit him with the pan in the side of the head with a downward chopping motion, like I was swinging an ax. Used both hands. Felt his skull cave. Crack.

George walked in. "What the fuck."

After George patched Paw Paw up the best he could we had to drop him off at the hospital. George kicked him out of the front seat;

didn't even really stop all the way. Dropped him off on the sidewalk close to the emergency room. He had two guys, Billy and Lil Steve clean up the hallway and get rid of Ray Ray's body. George said Ray Ray was hit so hard he was probably dead before he hit the ground. He patched up Paw Paw on our couch while I cleaned up the kitchen and living room. Billy and Lil Steve brought a big box of lawn trash bags, paper towels, and bleach industrial wipes. Luckily our place was all tile, so there was no carpet to deal with. Lil Steve and George took Paw Paw to the hospital while Billy and I cleaned the house. We had to put the couch cushions in the trash bags, too.

Thought Paw Paw was a goner.

Billy and I took all the bags downstairs to put them in the back of his old pick up truck. He had a camper shell on the bed so no one could see what he had back there. He opened the tailgate.

"Hurry up, nigga!"

As I threw the first bag in I noticed two bodies. Ray Ray... and Big Dil. Big Dil didn't make it.

"Hurry up!"

I threw the rest of the bags in as fast as I could.

"Now you owe George a favor."

What kind of favor? Why?

"What you mean *why*, boy? You think this shit is free? You think we like you, like a fucking charity or something? We do what we do because we don't want the cops snooping around here. We don't need outsiders around here snoopin' in our biz, ya dig? We take care of the people in this hood, but sometimes have to take out the garbage. Now you owe us. End of story."

The sun was coming up. I walked back upstairs and into the apartment. Mom was home. Oh fuck.

"Where my couch cushions, nigga? Why the building smell like bleach?"

Chapter 16,

Cole

Ma passed away when I was five. She had the cancer. Don't have too many memories of her. A few, I guess. Comfort. Warmth.

It's the only time in my life where I felt truly loved. Shame it was so long ago. They say what goes around comes around. Been waiting a long damn time. I hope it's true.

Pa was thirty when they met. He just came back from the war. Got shot too many times to go back for a fourth tour. Not even sure how him and Ma met. She was only eighteen at the time. Not even sure what she saw in him. He was a hard man. Drank a bit.

A man of few words, even back then.

I came along a year after they married. A year after that, baby brother showed up. He came down with the fever, and only lived a few months. Travis was his name. They buried Ma next to him in the cemetery by the old schoolhouse.

Pa never mentioned either one of them.

Ever.

Not sure how healthy that was for him.

Times were hard in those days and work was hard to come by. Pa went for stretches at a time without a job, but we got by. The drinking didn't help much. At all.

Pa loved drinking the whiskey. Old Crow was his brand. I smelled it once, smelled of death. He sat on the porch most nights with his bottle and a couple cans of chewing tobacco.

Guess you could say I was on my own.

Behind our trailer was farmland as far as the eye could see. Corn, wheat, beans, and the like.

I loved going out in them fields. I knew every field and every trail through the woods at least ten miles out in every direction. Maybe more.

About a mile out to the west there was this old barn, close to Highway Sixteen. My favorite place on the earth. My hideout. It was unusable for practical purposes. Weather and time had taken its toll like it does to all of us. I'd climb up in the loft and read my books and dirty magazines. Watch the cars go by. Sometimes smoke a cigarette if I could get one. Didn't have any friends that lived close by. If I did that's where I'd take 'em.

So one day around dusk I walk down to the barn. Fireflies were starting to come out, and I liked to catch 'em and put them in a jar.

There was a car parked next to the barn. Engine still running. Trunk open. I curiously walked forward. I was about twenty yards out or so and a big man in a suit came out of the main doors of the barn. He was dragging a little girl by the arm. She was younger than me. She kicked and flailed about. Tried to bite him. He shoved her to the ground. Hard.

I noticed he had a holster on his waist. The gun was shiny.

Another suit got out of the car. Also had a gun. They held her down and taped her mouth. Told her to shut the fuck up.

I was scared as hell. Froze. Didn't know what to do. I hid behind this big oak tree. Had to wait til they moved before I could go anywhere.

I peeked out. The suits grabbed her and went into the barn.

Headlights. Another car pulled off the highway on the dirt road towards the barn. I hit the dirt. The second car was about three feet away when it slowly passed me.

Two more suits. These ones had long guns of some kind. It was dark. Couldn't tell if they were rifles or shotguns. They walked through the main doors of the barn and shut them. I could hear some chatter, but nothing was audible. They had some light source, maybe a lantern. I could see lights and movements from shadows through the wooden slats on the side of the barn.

I ran as fast as I could back to Pa. Jumped up on the front porch. Pa was half a bottle down. Put in a dip, took a sip, and stared at me blankly as I caught my breath.

He leaned over and spat. "The fuck you runnin' for, boy?"

I told him what I had seen. It took a bit; I was still trying to catch my breath.

He took a long drink of the whiskey. Longer than usual. "You fuckin' wit me, boy?"

I informed him that I was not fucking with him.

"Watch your mouth, boy."

I yelled at him. It's the only time I've ever raised my voice at Pa. Pleaded with him. Told him we have to hurry and call the Nine One One. The cops can come and save her. It's the only way. We need to move now. Please, please put down the whiskey. We gotta move.

He slowly leaned over and spat again. "Yeah. Reckon you is right. Go on ahead now, boy, call them cops. It'll take 'em a bit to get out this way. They'll be able to clean this mess up. Go on in the back room and call 'em up. Hurry, now."

I ran back to Pa's room and made the call.

Nine one one, What is your emergency?

I told the dispatch lady the situation. At this point I was in tears. She asked for confirmation of my address and for exact directions to the barn. I told her the best that I could.

OK, now. I've dispatched officers to your location. You and your Daddy stay in your house, alright? And stay away from the barn.

I told her to hurry. Please.

I went out to the front porch to tell Pa. He wasn't there. I ran back inside towards the bathroom. I instinctively turned to the right. The wall didn't look normal.

The Mossberg was missing from the gun rack.

I ran towards the barn as fast as I could, but not fast enough. I could see it out in the distance. Tripped over a root. Hit the ground hard. Cut my hand up pretty good. I shook as I stood up. Legs frozen. I threw up. Everywhere.

Kept running.

Heard some yelling. Not sure what was said. I could hear Pa's voice for sure, deep, growly, and mad as hell.

Two gunshots.

Pistol rounds. Loud.

One gunshot.

Mossberg. Pa.

Pa. Living for the war he never talked about. Dreaming of the battle he could never return to.

And now it came to him.

For him.

Pa was crouched behind one of the cars, firing away into the barn. Hellfire came out of the barn hitting the car. One round hit Pa. He fell hard. He sat up. Reloaded. Charged the barn.

The whole ordeal maybe lasted thirty seconds. I could see the muzzle flashes from the gunfire through the slats of wood on the side of the barn. I thought it would never end.

And then silence.

Pa was still alive when I walked in. Getting shot ain't like in the movies. You know, where the hero says something noble and profound before twitching his head and passing peacefully to the other side.

I hesitated before I approached. Blood everywhere around Pa. His breathing was irregular. He was wheezing. Shaking. He couldn't move. I could see the pain in his face. He was shot in the gut a few times. Both hands were on his stomach attempting to apply pressure to the wounds. I noticed he was missing two fingers on his left hand. One of the suits lay next to him, dark blood still pouring out into the dirt.

After maybe a minute he was gone. If I could go back, I would've held his hand as he passed. Not even sure if he knew I was there.

I walked through the barn slowly. The others were shot to pieces. One had his innards spewed out at least ten feet or so, another had no head. The last man was still alive. He sat motionless, blinking every now and again. I was right in front of him, but he didn't look up. He was a really big fella. Sharply dressed. He must have tried to stop his leg from bleeding, but he knew his efforts were futile. He reached towards his ankle for a snub nose .38, but I wasn't afraid. He was in his own world. I almost felt bad for him. As I walked away I think he muttered something religious, maybe from the Bible, but I knew even God couldn't save him now.

The girl ran out from behind the remains of an old wagon. Into my arms. Crying. I picked her up. Told her it was all going to be OK. Told her she would be home soon. I took the tape off from around her head and carried her to the trailer. She passed out about halfway there. I could see the red and blue lights in the distance.

Pa was gone. Wasn't sure what to do.

He always had the answers.

Guess you could say now I was really on my own.

Pa's funeral was a small affair. A few of his buddies from the VFW showed up, along with some of the folk he worked with over the years. The pastor said some nice things. Read some comforting verses. Would've meant more if he actually knew Pa.

Pa was put in the ground next to Ma and baby brother. He didn't feel gone. It felt as if I could go back up to the trailer and there he'd be, drinking Old Crow and bitching about politics.

After the funeral I was moving out west to stay with an aunt I just met that day. Pa's sister. She didn't cry at the service. I thought she would.

An unfamiliar voice called my name. I turned.

"Come over here, kid."

He was a small man in a fine suit. New York accent. Intimidating presence. I didn't notice him at the funeral, but there he was. I walked over and looked down.

"Look at me, kid." I looked up. He put his hands on my shoulders. "You know who I am?"

I told him no.

"Doesn't matter who I am. Your dad saved my girl, you know that. I came to pay my respects, you know what I mean? More than that, I want to say thanks. Wish I could tell him thanks. Guy had some fuckin' stones on him, your dad. Look, I know nothing can replace him. Ever. But you need to know somethin'. These were some very bad people. Bad. And I heard you had to see all that. Sorry, but that's life, kid. Fucked up sometimes."

I looked back down.

"Here, take this." He handed me a business card. No name. No business. Just a handwritten phone number.

"You know who gets this number? Nobody. You ever need anything ever you call me, OK?"

I nodded yes. I still have the card. The numbers are faded, but I have it memorized.

I asked him what his daughter's name was.

"Maria."

I smiled through the pain of that day. Felt at peace.

That was Ma's name.

Chapter 17,

Paw Paw

So Robbie visited me in the old folk's home. I'm usually awake, but sometimes not all the way there. They say the blood loss hurt my brain, or something like that. My hair is all white now and I can walk slowly with a cane. Got a new roommate. His name is Ron, a sad fellow with no feet. Always seems tired.

My old roommate wasn't there anymore at the home. He was an official nut job.

This fucker's name was Frankie. Was a singer with a one-hit wonder about forty years ago. So I was only with this guy for a few days. Hated me. Despised me. Despised all blacks, actually. His family ended up paying extra so he could have his own room. The home had hired three new aides to help out with the influx of new patients. These new aides happened to be African American. And of course, Frankie knew they were out to get him. He was terrified. Never left his room day or night. All his meals had to be delivered to his room. He *always* talked about how the niggers were holding him down.

No one was holding him down. These guys were hired to clean, take out the trash, and help the patients get around.

But Frankie knew. He had to do something. He was like a Jew hiding in a Polish attic in 1939. They were going to get him. Maybe in his sleep? He couldn't take chances. Month after month he hid. He was too scared to leave his room. Couldn't sleep. Couldn't eat. Had bags under his eyes. Lost thirty pounds.

So Frankie escaped one morning. The alarm was triggered by the west exit by the parking lot. By the time the staff ran out he was gone. He had called a cab earlier and booked it out of the lot before anyone could catch him. He ended up at the grocery store and bought a few items.

One watermelon. One bottle of gin. One butcher knife.

In the parking lot of the grocery store he downed the bottle of gin. Straight down the hatch. He was then driven back to the nursing home. He had seen so many employees go through the front door he knew the keypad code to get in. Joan happened to be in the restroom at the time. He went straight to the cafeteria.

Frankie set up shop at the first empty table he could find. It was breakfast, so most of the residents were there. He put down the watermelon and started hacking away.

Chop.

Chop.

Chop.

The slices were uneven, some were just mush. Melon juice was everywhere. His shirt. His face. The table. The floor.

Chop.

Chop.

Chop.

An old lady rolled up in a wheelchair. She took a slice. "Thanks Frankie." She smiled as she rolled away. She went back to her table and ate the melon, making a big fucking mess.

Others lined up. They all grabbed a piece and went back to their tables. Meanwhile the staff tried to approach Frankie. They didn't get too close, though.

Chop.

Chop.

Chop.

He yelled at the three African American aides.

"You want to rob joy from me don't you, boys! Want to fuck up everything I've done! You think you're so smart don't you! Try it motherfucker! Try it!"

They asked him politely to put the knife down. Melon juice dripped all over the cafeteria.

Frankie held his knife out at the aides. He began to sing. He still had his voice.

The cafeteria fell silent.

He sang:

"Oh beautiful!

For spacious skies!

And amber waves of grain!

The purple mountain majesties,

Above the fruited plain!

America!

America!

God shed his grace on thee.

And crown thy good,

with brotherhood,

From sea to shining sea!"

The cafeteria erupted in applause. Frankie smiled.

"I can still sing, and I can still whip a nigger's ass! Meet me outside, boys, if you're man enough." Frankie drunkenly waddled out to the nearest exit and walked to the middle parking lot. He chucked the butcher knife as far as he could, turned around, and put up his fists.

As he turned, the three aides were there. Baffled. Confused.

"Put 'em up boys. Or are you niggers too afraid to dance?"

The 'fight' didn't go in Frankie's favor. They took him down in about half a second. He screamed and flailed. Like a turtle on its back.

And for the first time in Frankie's life, the blacks kept him down.

Chapter 18,

Jeff

My favorite memory of her started off with no plans at all. We woke up together on a Sunday morning. My roommate was out of town so we had the place to ourselves. I made breakfast while she slept in. Coffee, eggs, bacon, and English Muffins. English Muffins were her favorite.

Taking the comforter, she migrated from the bed to the living room couch. She looked like a slow moving upside down ice cream cone. We ate breakfast and curled up on the couch for hours watching Seinfeld. For lunch we called in some Chinese food. She always ordered Orange Chicken. Come to think of it, I always order Orange Chicken now.

After lunch? We took a break and headed back to the bedroom. As the song says, sky rockets in flight, afternoon delight.

When we finished she went to her purse. Said she had something to show me. She tossed me an old coin. I asked her if it was payment for my recently rendered services. She punched me in the arm.

I went over to the window to get a better look at the coin. It was a little bronze coin with faded Roman numerals around the edges and some Roman official on it. She said her dad gave it to her randomly when she was little. Gracie wasn't sure where he got it from.

So we sat at my computer desk and began to hunt the interwebs for any information. She sat on my lap in this awkward-looking yet comfortable entanglement and we looked for hours. Pages and pages of different coins from different eras.

And then we found it. She screamed. I jumped for joy. She kissed me.

A hero for that brief moment in time.

The coin was from the Mint of Rome, circa 270-275 AD. Worth about eight hundred dollars.

Then we went back to bed, but there wasn't much sleeping if you catch my drift.

And that was it. My perfect day. So simple and unplanned. Food, Seinfeld, more food, sex, and ancient currency from the era of Caesar Lucius Domitius Aurelianus Augustus, and more sex.

It's been years since we've seen each other, or even had contact. I don't even remember why we broke up. I do remember not being too broken up about it at the time. My roommate took me out on the town. We probably got smashed and I ended up getting some strange from a fatty. I foolishly thought that I would easily find another girl that connected with me like she did. But as the years went by I never found the same connection. I always wondered what would have happened if we'd stayed together. I secretly hoped I would run into her at a store since I was reasonably sure we still lived in the same city. I practiced what I would say if that moment ever happened. And if I did would she be single? Would I say the right thing?

I tried looking her up on social media, but I knew she wouldn't be there. She never had any online profiles. Her dad didn't let her when she was younger. Said it was for her safety. She wouldn't talk about her dad that much and I never pushed the issue. I only met him once during lunch at some diner. He was the biggest, scariest person I've ever met. I think he had a gun under his jacket, but I couldn't tell for sure. He didn't say a word to me. Her mother was kind, though.

One day I sat down and wrote her a letter. I didn't have anywhere to send it.

Dear Gracie,
Hey there! It's been too long since we've
talked. I always wondered how your
life was going. I recently was thinking about
the good times we had in the all
or nothin' days, as you called them. I'm
still with the same firm. It'll be seven
years this September. Has it really been that
long? Also, I live in North Smithton
now. Recently bought a house by Smally
Lake. Hope this letter finds you and
finds you well. Write me back!
-Jeff

I put the letter on the front counter and didn't do anything with it for about two weeks. It just sat there looking at me. Haunting me.

The next Friday I found her mom's name and an address online. Grabbed an envelope and put a stamp on it. I dropped it in a mailbox on the way to work. I tried to get it back, but my arm was too big to reach down the slot. It was gone. I wondered if she'd get the letter. Did her parents still live there? Did she still live in the same area? Should I have written down my phone number? Would she think I'm crazy for trying to contact her after all these years?

Too many variables.

Too many questions.

Whatever happens happens.

* * *

About a week went by and I revived a small padded envelope in the mail. From Gracie. My heart skipped a beat. I opened it right by the mailbox.

> *Jeff! OMG Mom called and told me you*
> *wrote a letter! Who in the hell writes*
> *letters anymore? You're still so old fashioned.*
> *Of course I still think about the*
> *all or nothin' days! They were the best.*
> *All good memories. Things were so*
> *much simpler then. I do miss you! We should*
> *get lunch sometime and catch up*
> *for sure! Bad news, dad passed away*
> *about six years ago. Good news, I've*
> *been married now for almost three years!*
> *My husband owns a construction*

company and it's doing well. I spend my days
watching our two-year-old, Walter.
He is a handful! Bet you never thought I
would have kids! Ha! Times change, I
guess. Taped in the envelope is a piece of the
all or nothin' days! Congrats on the
new house. It was great to hear from you.
Hugs, Gracie

I reached in the envelope and pulled the tape back. A coin fell out.

From the mint of Rome. Circa 270- 275 AD.

Chapter 19,

Gracie's Dad

I still had my backup gun.

Thirty-eight Special.

Fully loaded.

Six rounds.

I look out at the four men around me. They're all shot to pieces, including me. It's hard to move my neck. It's hard to breathe. I see him, the man that shot me. He's still breathing, at least for now.

Strange to think we were all alive a few minutes ago.

Strange to think we'll all be dead in a few minutes.

See you on the other side, you fuck.

I'm thinking about my life now. The pain is starting to numb. Thinking about closing my eyes and not opening them up again. My wife collapsing in the kitchen when she gets the call. My daughter hugging and sobbing to her shit loser boyfriend when she gets the news.

It all happened so sudden. This drunken grizzly looking motherfucker shows up with a shotgun, starts yelling, and before I can say anything he starts unloading on us. Dropped all four of us in less than twenty seconds. We tried to fire back, and I eventually tagged him, but he was mad. Insane. Unstoppable. He ran at us like he had a death wish.

A request I gladly granted.

I don't know where he came from. We weren't followed, and no one knew where the hiding place was except for me and Mac over there, and I know Mac ain't no rat. If by some miracle of a chance he ratted us after twenty years of working together, it didn't matter now. The first two shots hit him in the face. Closed casket funeral for him. They could save some dough by getting a shorter casket seeing how he don't have a head no more.

For some reason I'm now thinking about my Uncle Jackie. He was a devout Christian. Had the true faith. Went to church every Sunday. Told everyone he knew about the gospel of Christ. He knew the facts. Jesus, born of a virgin, performed miracles, walked around with his disciples, and died for your sins on the cross only to be raised again on the third day to live in heaven forever and ever. Accept Jesus into your heart and forever reap the heavenly rewards of the afterlife singing praises to the King of Kings for all eternity.

Amen.

Religion never took to me, though. I never found it believable. And I did try, believe me. Sat there every Sunday in the front row with my wife for the last twenty five years. Listening. Hearing. Praying. Repenting. Asking for forgiveness. Waiting for the spirit to fill me.

Even in the end, I'm still waiting.

Seeing nothing.

Hearing nothing.

Feeling nothing.

Maybe my sins are just too big.

And now that it's all over I'm left wondering what's on the other side. I'll find out soon enough.

Uncle Jackie always talked about the Book of Job. His favorite. Job was steadfast and true. Never doubted God. Never questioned. And in the end he received all of God's blessings. All because he never cursed God in his trials.

Not that I'm cursing God now.

Can't curse what you don't believe in.

I was leaning against the inside barn wall. I sat down. Gently. Dropped my rifle. I slowly unbuckled my belt. I was shot in the leg and bleeding out everywhere. Wrapped the belt around my leg as a makeshift tourniquet. It may slow the bleeding, but I know I'm only delaying the inevitable.

He also shot me in the chest twice. God, he was fast. Never seen anything like it. He must have had military training. I had my vest on which did stop the penetration, but I know I have internal bleeding and broken ribs.

The boys in blue were on their way, I was sure of it. I didn't have enough strength to run. I didn't have enough strength to hide. Shooting my way out would be futile.

Still thinking about Uncle Jackie and his faith. Still thinking about all his talks on Job, but my mind wanders to the other characters in the story.

This is a tale that's so different from the rest of the bible. I'm not even sure why it's there to begin with. No one even knows who the author is. It just... exists.

Like me for the next few minutes.

We start out with Satan and God hanging out. Just hanging out casually drinking tea. For some reason God and Satan talk about Job. Job is God's most faithful human. Nothing could make Job turn his back on Almighty God.

Nothing?

Satan asks God to lower his protection on Job. He reasons that the only reason Job is faithful is because God has blessed him with so many riches. Take Job's shit away and he'll curse you.

Guaranteed.

Let's hurt Job a little.

Let's put him to the test.

Let's play a game, just for fun.

So God gets in on the action. Tells Satan, "OK, mess him up. Hurt him. Just don't kill him."

And Old Red Horns turns the screws in on this poor motherfucker. The man that has never sinned gets punished for doing everything right.

Satan kills his kids.

His livestock.

His crops.

And just for fun gives him a terrible illness.

In all these trials Job never curses God. He never once complains. Even his wife tells him to curse God and die. Of course she didn't die. She's still around to nag him to no end.

Uncle Jackie always referenced Job when things went wrong.

"God is testing you when things go bad."

"Satan is trying to weaken you in these trials"

"Job is an example of how to act and how to be."

Uncle Jackie had such passion and conviction.

But in God and Satan's game Job is not the only human character.

If I have to believe this story then I have to believe that Job's kids were *actual* people. Actual people sacrificed in a twisted distance pissing contest between God and Satan. Killed just so God could say, "Told ya so." All his kids killed just for fun. To win a bet.

So if all of it is all real and that's what happened back then, how do I know it doesn't happen today?

Fun games.

Funny ha ha.

Games. And if you're not the lead in the play you're expendable. All of your joys and sorrows for years ending in an untimely death just to test someone else.

I ask myself, am I one of Job's kids? Is my death going to further test someone else? Who is the Job in my life? Will God get to say, "Told ya so?"

Naked I came from my mother's womb. Naked I shall depart.

The Lord hath given and the Lord hath taken away.

I uttered these words out loud. Probably my last. Watched a shadow go past.

Is death on my tail?

We all start out the same. Helpless. Crying. Shitting ourselves. The church teaches that babies are born into darkness. Into sin. But I don't think so. Some grow up and turn out to be good people. Decent people. Others...bad apples? Turn into the five of us here.

I think of my wife, Martha.

I think of my daughter, Gracie.

My girls.

I'm starting to fade, but it feels like I'm waking up from a dream. A dream so good I need to fall back asleep and see where it takes me. I hope it takes me into the light. I hope it's like they say. A better place. You get to see loved ones. Be at peace. What I wouldn't give to hug my ma again. What I wouldn't give to see my dad and give him a nice right cross on the chin.

Noise.

Shuffling.

Voices.

Oh fuck.

Fuck me.

As the blue and red lights close in I fade a bit more.

I bend my left leg up and reach for my ankle holster the best I can.

Almost there. You can do it. Almost, baby. So hard to move this fucking leg. God help me. Drag the leg back. Reach forward. Drag the leg back. Oh shit. There it is. The handle. Pull. Pull. Got it. Lean back. Breathe. Thank God. After all this time, a prayer answered. Maybe there is hope.

I have my backup gun.

Dad's old thirty-eight special.

First gun I ever shot.

Last gun I'll ever shoot.

Fully loaded.

Six rounds.

But I only need one.

Epilogue,

Robbie

Mom's been gone now for about two weeks. Sometimes she does this, but last time when she left she looked bad. I've always prepared myself for the day she wouldn't return and what I'd tell baby brother. I had to have a plan, though, to get us out of here.

Look, I'm not proud of this, but I got to survive. I started snatching purses. I'd skip school and take the train downtown and wait. See some older lady with a nice bag, run up and snatch it as fast as I could. Never got caught. Chased a few times by bystanders, but I was too fast.

I only did that a few times though. No one carries that much cash anymore. The most I ever got was seventy bucks. Once there was a watch, but only got a twenty for it. I needed to make big bread. Get me and little brother out of here. To a different city. Start over.

So I went to George. George said I owed him two jobs. One job for patching up Paw Paw and one for getting rid of Ray Ray's body.

"Found a job for you, young nigga. Did a little traveling to the suburbs, hanging around the grocery stores. Went in, bought a snack from the bakery, cup of coffee, and sat in the lot. Just waited. And then I saw it. A big, beautiful, brand new pick up truck. Lifted, rims, the whole works."

You want me to steal the truck?

"No no no. It wasn't the truck, itself. It was what was *on* the truck. See, while we gotta hide our guns, these fools openly flaunt them. These Don't Tread On Me, NRA, Second Amendment, Blue Lives Matter motherfuckers. He got all these bumper stickers on the back of his pick up truck. A matter of fact, he came out the grocery store with a pistol on his hip. Open carry motherfucker. Actually waved to the police officer that was at the entrance. *Waved*, no shit. Now, open carry is legal in this state, but can you imagine what would happen if I waved to the police with a Glock on my hip? You out your goddamned mind. Them niggas execute me on site."

So what is the job? I don't get it.

"I'll tell you what the job is. I cased the fool back to his house; Lives out in the country. No neighbors for about a quarter mile. He goes to work every day, leaves at seven. I got the address, you take my truck, break in, get all his guns. Now I'm fair, so I'll pay you a premium for each gun. Clean that redneck out."

How you know he's got a lot of guns? What if he only has a few?

"Nigga, I can feel it. In my bones. The big truck, the open carry; I can guarantee you he's got a armory down there. And I want you to bring Young Charles with you."

Isn't he kind of young for a job like this?

"Well that's why they call him Young Charles ain't it now, nigga?

* * *

We went out to the country on a Friday morning. He didn't have many guns in the house, only a shotgun under the bed and a revolver in the nightstand drawer. I started to lose hope.

"Hey Robbie, what about that shed out back?"

It was locked with a small Masterlock. I used the crowbar we used to break in the house to try and bust it off. It didn't break, but the whole latch assembly fell to the ground along with the lock. Young Charles and I stepped in. I reached up and pulled the chain. The bulb lit up. Our jaws dropped. On the left was a workbench with all kinds of tools and machines. At the end of it, two boxes of silencers. The wall in front of the bench was covered with Army posters and American Flags. The rest of the walls were mounted with guns. Every gun you could ever think of. On the ground were boxes and boxes of bullets and magazines. I backed George's pick up truck to the door of the shed and we cleaned it all out. Two hundred seven guns total, plus the silencers, ammo, and magazines. Put a tarp over the merchandise and got the hell out of there. I thought something was wrong with the truck because it was hard to move at first, but it was just the weight. The bed of the truck sagged and I had to floor it all the way back, even though I couldn't drive that fast.

We went back to George's garage.

"The fuck you niggas do to my back tires? They damn near flat."

He opened the back.

"Oh fuck. Good job, boys. Good job."

Two days later George gave me ten thousand dollars.

"You did good, Robbie. Real good. Unbelievable payday."

How much did you get for all of it?

"Well, I've only sold some of it. Let's put it this way; I just handed you ten grand, and it doesn't even look like the pile was touched."

Am I gonna get any more bread, then?

"Fuck you, nigga. You lucky I gave you that. You still owe me one job, though. I'll make you a deal. You do this next job and I'll give you another ten grand."

What's the job?

* * *

Ten grand more? That's enough to get me and little brother out for real. Take care of him. Give him some sort of chance in this world. I was a little nervous about this job, though.

George wanted a car. A newer ride. With the keys, so that means I got to carjack. Never done that before. The intersection I'm at right now is notorious for this long stoplight. Everyone hates it. People used to run it, but now it's got a camera on it. So all I got to do is wait for the right car. Fuck, it's cold out here. I had four shooters of whiskey that I downed to give me a little edge, but I took them on an empty stomach and am starting to feel a bit buzzed. I had a revolver with me, the one that I found in the redneck's nightstand. I kept that one for myself.

George wanted a nice, big car. Preferably an Impala or something similarly sized. And there it was! The perfect car! A big, beautiful, black Lincoln. Please stop at the light. Please get the red light. Please get the red light. Please get the red light.

He got the red light.

His window was already down! Perfect. A really big older white guy in a suit. It was so cold out. Why was his window down? Who cares. I ran up. Stuck my gun in the car. He slowly put his hand up. Shit, his daughter was in the car, wouldn't have taken this car if I knew she was here. She was so pretty, a little younger than me. Scared out of her mind. It's okay, they'll get out.

"Take it easy, fella. We're getting out. You take the car. Take the money. Take it, we're not going to be any trouble."

Thank God. Probably really nice people. Felt bad for the guy. His car was mint, too. But I got to do what I got to do.

I'm just glad this is going to be easy.

Everything is going to be okay now.